Bartley's Man

Paula Goodlett and Gorg Huff

D1707665

2016 Eric Flint's Ring of Fire Press
Copyright © 2016 by Paula Goodlett and Gorg Huff
All rights reserved.
ISBN 9781537052335

Cover Art by: Laura Givens

OTHER RING OF FIRE PRESS PUBLICATIONS

Arrested Development

As Ye Have Done It Unto one of the Least

Blood in Erfurt

Essen Defiant

Essen Steel

Gloom Despair and Agony on You

Incident in Alaska Prefecture

Joseph Hanauer

Letters Home

Love and Chemistry

Medicine and Disease after the Ring of Fire

Muse of Music

No ship for Tranquebar

Second Chance Bird

Storm Signals

The Battle for Newfoundland

The Danish Scheme

The Demons of Paris

The Evening of the Day

The Heirloom

The Play's the Thing

The Society of Saint Philip of the Screwdriver

Turn Your Radio On

Paula Goodlett and Gorg Huff

Table of Contents

Chapter 1 — Old Soldier

June 30, 1631
Tilly's Tercio, Outside Badenburg

ohan Kipper was hungover again, and that was good. For Johan, going into battle with a hangover was almost as good as going into battle a little drunk. It distracted him from what he had to do. He squinted as the morning sun stabbed his brain through his eyes and then shifted his pike just a little. He was in the second rank of pikes and happy enough to be there. It was a respectable position but not as dangerous as the front rank.

Johan shuffled forward, holding up his pike. They were here to teach Badenburg not to close its gates against Tilly's army and to deal with the strangers that, rumor had it, were wizards and witches. Johan snorted and his brain rattled in his head. He winced at the pain. *Wizards? This is the seventeenth century.*

The tercio was moving forward, and he was busy enough just keeping his feet moving and his head from falling off. He didn't have time to worry about putting his pike through someone or having someone put theirs through him. So he barely noticed the difference in the sounds. The enemy, at least the group in front of him, fired one ragged volley and turned and ran. Just as well. He probably wasn't up to much of a fight.

Then Johan was bumped. He turned and Karl, the sniveling little shit, had dropped his pike. Then he saw the blood that came from Karl's mouth and the new hole in Karl's side. Karl was a pup, and arrogant

3

besides, *but damn!* They were in the second rank, near the middle, and Karl had still been hit in the side, hard enough to knock him into Johan.

Things went downhill from there. An army, even part of Tilly's army, could only take so much, and this one was being cut to pieces from so far away that they couldn't fight back. It took a while, but it started to crumble. Then it broke. All of a sudden everyone was running, and Johan was running with them. But not very far. He was too hung over and, well, just too damned old to run as far as he needed to go.

After a few minutes, and on the other side of the baggage train, he stopped. He might have kept running, but he was on the wrong side of fifty, hung over, and wearing a heavy buff coat. If the damn cavalry killed him, at least it would stop his head aching. Huffing and puffing, Johan waited for the cavalry to catch him. His hands were already up when they got there.

July 1, 1631
Power Plant

Darlene Myers looked again at the device sitting on her work table. *I'm not a god-damned electrical engineer. I'm a tech. I don't fucking design dials, I read dials. This isn't fair.*

Darlene tried not to cry. She had been in a state of shock right after the Ring of Fire, but that was fading now. Now every time she looked up or anything went wrong she started bawling like a two-year-old. This time it was the circuitry in the gauge, a sensor that measured the speed of the alternating current. It was used to adjust draw, to feed more or less power into holding, and to keep output in balance. It also had a small integrated circuit that they couldn't reproduce. They needed some sort of old-fashioned timing circuit. Maybe a tuning fork. But Darlene didn't have a clue how a tuning fork timer worked. She looked again at the tiny circuit board sitting on the scratched work table.

Darlene hadn't even noticed that the town of Grantville had troops in the field. She was too caught up in her grief. If Julie Marie hadn't made me work that Sunday, I would have been home with Johnny and Jack. I never would have gotten caught in the Ring of Fire.

July 3, 1631
Grantville P.O.W. Holding Area

Johan Kipper had been afraid before each and every battle he had ever fought, and there had been many. But this was different. For one thing, this was after the battle, and he wasn't waiting to fight. He was waiting to be judged. He was to be judged by a camp follower. He didn't know the Gretchen girl well. Hardly at all. But she was the one to judge him, and that was scary. Johan was not a very good man and he knew it. He was a mean drunk, and he knew that too.

There weren't many people who were held in more contempt than soldiers, but camp followers were. They had been the only safe outlet for the anger he felt at the way his life had turned out. At least they had seemed to be safe. Now Johan was afraid, in a way that he had never been afraid before.

What made Johan a little different from some of his fellow soldiers was that he realized what scared him. Not that he would be treated unfairly, but that he would be treated as he deserved.

He had started out as a soldier forty years ago at the age of fifteen. Absolutely sure he would become a captain. Ten years later, after having survived smallpox, he had hoped to become a sergeant. Now, he didn't even want to be a soldier anymore, but he didn't know anything else. His family had been in service: servants to a wealthy merchant in Amsterdam. He had run off to be a soldier.

Johan was fifty-four years and spoke a smattering of half a dozen languages. He was five feet six inches tall, had graying brown hair and six teeth, four uppers and two lowers. He had the typical pockmarks that denoted a survivor of smallpox, a scar running down the left side of his face . . . and he was tired. Tired of fighting, tired of killing, and scared of dying.

He was surprised that he wasn't one of the ones who got his picture on a piece of paper and told to get out of the New United States. He was less surprised, almost comforted, by the lecture he got about getting drunk and hitting people. The lecture amounted to "Don't Do It. We can always take another picture and print another wanted poster, if we need to."

When offered a place in the army, he respectfully declined. When asked what he was qualified to do, he said he had been in service once. He had to explain what he meant. "My family were servants in Amsterdam." He was assigned to a labor gang.

July 6, 1631
Delia Higgins' House

Johan Kipper wasn't in manacles as they drove up. They weren't needed. There was a heavy screen between the back seat where Johan was seated and the front where the "Police Chief" drove the device and the doors in the back section of the self-powered cart didn't open from the inside. They pulled off the paved street through a wide gate made of the gray metal that the up-timers had in such abundance. Once through the gate, they were on a short paved road. On one side of the road was a house in the style the up-timers preferred and just beside it one of the narrow, boxy houses that they called "mobile homes." Across the way there was a "parking lot" like the one at the school, but considerably smaller. Behind and further down the street were row on row of white painted boxes.

The car stopped in front of the more normal-looking house and Police Chief Dan Frost turned to face Johan through the screen. "We've talked about your drinking and you know we can make up a wanted poster easy enough. You know you're getting an opportunity here because you speak some English. So I'm just going to repeat this last part so you don't forget. I don't want to hear you've caused Mrs. Higgins any trouble. She's a nice lady and will treat you right. I expect you to show her respect. If I hear you've given her any problems, any problems at all, you'll regret it."

Then the police chief got out of the car and opened the back door so Johan could get out. It wasn't that easy. The couches in these carts were incredibly comfortable, but they were hard to get into and out of. All the while, bouncing around in his mind, were the words "Delia Higgins is a Lady." Delia Higgins was an up-timer noble.

Carrying his woolen cap in his hands, as was proper when brought before a Lady, he followed Police Chief Dan Frost into the living room. Lady Higgins was about five seven inches tall. She had black hair going to gray, and dark eyes. And she didn't look happy.

The police chief introduced him, and with a hand to his cap took his leave.

"Sit down, Mr. Kipper." She waved him to a couch upholstered in a light brown fabric. She went to a big chair, a throne really, that was upholstered in leather. "Kipper? That's an English name, isn't it?"

"My grandda was English, ma'am," Johan said, taking a careful seat on the couch.

She looked around, then her mouth tightened and she turned back to him. "I'm sorry, Mr. Kipper. I'm out of practice at hiring people." She took a deep breath. "What I need is more than just a night watchman. I need a connection to this century. We have some things to do, and to do them we need someone who speaks the language and more." She stood abruptly, and Johan jumped up in alarm.

"Come with me. I'll show you around the place while we talk."

They went out the front door, which she opened before he could get to it to open it for her, and they were on the front porch. It was wooden and covered. Down the steps from it was a green lawn and flowerbeds filled with flowers to make an Amsterdam tulip collector green with envy. Not that they were tulips. There were roses, bigger roses than Johan had ever seen in his life, and more fragrant too. There were daisies and other flowers he couldn't put a name to. Lady Higgins led him down the steps, pointing out the beds and naming the flowers.

Then they proceeded down the walk and went to the "office," as she called it. It was the mobile home.

The door they entered was across from a counter. There was a woman behind the counter who was introduced as Ramona Higgins. She seemed nervous, but Johan didn't have much time to notice. To their left was an opening and Lady Higgins led him that way. The opening was a hall and on one side there was a sink and cabinets. "This is the kitchen," Lady Higgins said. On the other side of the hall was a white box that Lady Higgins opened and cold air came out. The box was mostly filled with the bottled drinks that the up-timers called sodas, but there was also a plate with the clear plastic they used over **it** and a meal under the plastic. Meat, vegetables, and what looked like some kind of mashed something.

"This is the fridge. We'll get the sodas out of here to give you more room, but mostly you will be eating with the family." She pointed to another box, a smaller one sitting on the cabinet. "That's the microwave. Don't put metal in it. In fact, don't use it. Not till we've had a chance to teach you what is and isn't safe to put in it." She pointed again. "This is the stove, but it's not hooked up to gas. Plates and glasses are in the cabinets." She opened them and showed him. She got out a glass, went to the sink, and turned a handle. Water came out and flowed down the drain. She filled the glass and handed it to him. Then she gestured for him to drink.

It was water, clear and cold. Johan hoped he wouldn't get the runs. That often happened when you drank water, rather than wine or beer. She held out her hand. He gave her the glass and she emptied it into the sink.

Then placed it upside down in a rack to drain, making it clear what the rack was for. She opened the other doors and cabinets showing him what was in them. She pointed at a green painted cabinet with shiny silver trim. "That's the dishwasher, but it's not hooked up either. If we need to we can get a plumber out here to hook it up, but we'll wait on that. As I mentioned, you will be eating with the family most of the time."

Out the other end of the kitchen hall was another room. It had a small table and two chairs but was mostly filled with the paper boxes that the up-timers seemed to favor. She waved vaguely. "The dining room. We've been using it for storage. We'll move this stuff out to one of the storage containers on the lot. You're probably going to have to do that." She led him through the dining room into another room. It too was full of boxes. "We'll clean out the bedroom for you, Mr. Kipper. Honestly, you'll probably end up doing that, but I'll get David to help you. David and Donny are my grandsons. They and their mother live with me. My son, Dalton, and his family are in town but don't live at the lot. So, tell me about yourself, Mr. Kipper."

Johan was uncomfortable every time she called him Mister. He'd never been a Mister in his life, so he started by saying, "Just Johan is enough, or Kipper. You don't need to call me Mister, ma'am. I was born on an estate not fifteen miles from Amsterdam and lived there until I was fifteen. Then I ran off to be a soldier and make my fortune. It didn't turn out so well." He went on to give her an outline of his life as a soldier and the various posts he'd held. He'd never gotten very high, but he had been an officer's aide a few times and she seemed pleased with that. The strange thing was that she seemed honestly interested in him, in what his life had been like.

She led him back to the dining room and through another door. This one led to a confusing place. She pointed out the washing machine that was too small to bathe in. The dryer, a metal box a lot like the dishwasher.

The bathroom sink, which he understood, the toilet, which he had seen in the refugee center, and the bathtub that was almost long enough to lie down in.

∞ ∞ ∞

Delia Higgins had expected a local, not a soldier in the invading army. The interview was uncomfortable for her.

Delia was looking for more than a night watchman. She needed a link to this time and place. She needed someone who could help her find a buyer for the dolls so she could finance David and his friends' building a sewing machine. She had promised them that, and now that the bank had refused the loan, selling her dolls was the only way she could think of to get the money. She didn't say that, not just yet. She wasn't sure she trusted the ugly little man.

Johan's appearance bothered her. First, because by any modern standard, he was a remarkably ugly man. Mostly that was because of his bad teeth and the pockmarks. By the standards of his time, he was the low end of average. Second, because part of what she needed was someone who could speak to the down-timers for her. She hired him, but she wasn't happy about it.

The agreement was maintenance and one hundred dollars a month. Really poor pay, but all Delia felt she could afford. As for the job, Johan would live in the "office," and he would be expected to make at least four walking inspections of the lot each night. There would be occasional errands for him to run. Long hours but light work.

∞ ∞ ∞

For Johan, the interview was much worse. She asked her questions. He answered them in his somewhat broken English. She asked more questions, seeking clarification. This woman looked at him, really looked. She didn't examine him like he was a horse or a dog she was thinking of buying. She really saw him. She acknowledged him like he was a real person. Complex, capable of thought. As if he had value. She was, as the English might say: "Neither fish nor fowl nor good red meat." He could not find a place in his world where she belonged. What made it worse, almost intolerably worse, was that he fully realized that it was her world that mattered now, not his. And if he couldn't even find where she fit, how was he to find where he fit?

She had, as far as he could see, the wealth and power of a prosperous townswoman, but she did not act right. She didn't scorn. Johan was not a stupid man. He understood better than most what the arrival of a town from the future meant. He realized that the rules had changed. That these people could do things that no one else could do.

For instance, despite the fact that she seemed apologetic about it, the "maintenance" turned out to be much more than Johan expected. There was an indoor flush toilet and a shower. To Delia Higgins, "maintenance" included *her* paying for *his* health and dental care. It also included uniforms for work and at least some clothing for off work. It included eating as well as any member of her family did, and his own room, and a bathroom, because they had never removed the bathroom fittings from the "mobile home" —which acted as an office.

Johan was not an evil man, though he often thought he was. For fifty-four years, with one exception, he had kept his place, knowing full well that stepping out of it could mean his death. That's a lot of habit. The thing about chains is they're secure. They're safe. You get used to them. Then you get to depend on them. Johan had worn the chains of lower-class existence his whole life. He didn't know how to walk without their weight.

July 7, 1631
Higgins' Storage Lot

From the first, Johan noticed that Master David Bartley, Lady Higgins' grandson, was watching him. He made his rounds of the storage lot, walking along the chainlink fence and making sure that there were no holes or places where someone might crawl under or climb over, which was helped by the barbed wire that topped the fence. Johan was impressed by barbed wire. Then Johan went down the rows of containers, checking the locks on all of them and opening the unlocked ones to make sure **there** was nothing hiding in them.

Through it all, David Bartley was around. Not quite following him, but always there. It wasn't very subtle, and it was clear to Johan that David wasn't well practiced at sneaking about.

Johan tipped his cap to the young lordling whenever it was obvious that he had seen him, but the rest of the time he pretended not to notice.

Finally the lad came up to him. "Yes, sir, Master David?"

"Well, ah, I just wanted to see how you're getting along."

"Well enough, sir," Johan said. "The bed in the mobile home is wonderful soft. And breakfast was fine."

"Good then. What do you know about manufacturing?"

Johan tried not to show how nervous he was. The question seemed a trap, and one he couldn't help but fall into. "Almost nothing, sir. I've been a soldier most of my life and was in service before that."

That took a bit of explanation. Young Master David didn't know what "in service" meant.

They talked most of the afternoon.

They talked about battles and captains, about work and honor. Then it slipped out. "Ye don't act right, ye up-timers," Johan said. He wanted the words back as soon as they were out, but the young master didn't seem upset.

He just asked, "How should we act?"

"Ye don't act yer proper place! Sorry, Master David, for speaking out of turn."

The young master looked at him with a considering air, then spoke with an authority that Johan couldn't ignore. "No. You've said too much, or not enough, and this may be something we need to know."

Johan fumbled with the words. "Like I said, sir. Ye don't act yer place. One minute ye're one thing and the next another. Ye talk like a banker, or a merchant, or a lord or craftsman, or, oh, I don't know. Ye talk to me the same way ye'd talk to yer president."

Master David started to say something, then stopped and said something else. "How should we act? If you were hired by a lord or a merchant, how would they act?"

Johan told him. He mentioned John George of Saxony, who called for a beer by pouring the dregs of his last beer over the servant's head. But mostly he focused on the way the nobles and important townsmen would look past you and talk to the air as if you weren't real, but just a thing.

"That's—" Master David said, and stopped. He looked at Johan and Johan could see the condemnation in his eyes. For a moment he thought it was directed at him. Johan was afraid then, afraid that it was all some sort of elaborate trap and he would be put out for impertinence, have his picture on a wanted poster, and have to run for his life.

"God. They must be terrified of you," David said, and Johan couldn't quite take it in. It made no sense. Then the lad started laughing. Free and easy, like he'd just heard the funniest joke of all time. To Johan it seemed that he was the joke. He didn't know what it was all about, and he was scared and angry all at once. But Johan was an old man who had lived his entire life at the bottom rung of his world. Scared was very strong and it beat angry to a bloody pulp.

It took a little while for David Bartley to get himself under control. Long enough so that anger had been completely put down and Johan was just scared.

Then the lad stopped laughing and said, "I'm sorry, Johan, but your face. Looking at me like I was crazy."

That was even harder to take. A young lord like Master Bartley didn't apologize to the likes of Johan Kipper. Wouldn't apologize to someone like Johan if they had a knife at his throat and a blunderbuss in his belly. But David Bartley apologized and did it easy, like Johan was owed an apology, and it was the most natural thing in the world for him to give it.

Then he said something even crazier. "I am not afraid of you." Master David said it clearly, honestly, and without the least trace of fear. "I don't have to trap you into doing something that would be an excuse to punish you. I don't need to make you weak to feel strong, or safe. That's why we act the way we do, Johan! The way that seems so wrong to you. Because we are not afraid. Not the way these German lords are, and because we are not afraid of you, you don't have to be afraid of us.

"Here is how you should act around us. Do your job as well as you can. State your views freely. If you think I am doing something wrong, say so. I may or may not follow your advice, but I won't punish you for giving it. I promise you that. Can you do that, Johan? If you can, you will have a place here. For as long as we can make one for you."

Johan wanted to cry. David Bartley bought himself a man with those words. The lad might not know it yet, but Johan did. Johan might be an old dog of a soldier, but he was David Bartley's old dog, now and forever. For Johan wanted to know how to be unafraid like young Master David. So very unafraid that he could be kind. Or if he couldn't learn it, at least to be around it.

After Master David left, Johan thought about the afternoon. "I am not afraid of you," the young master had said, and Johan had to believe. *And the lords are.* As he thought about it, Johan believed that too.

July 7, 1631
Delia Higgins' Sewing Room

Johan Kipper looked at the Singer sewing machine in total confusion. It wasn't that Johan was stupid, or even ignorant. It was simply that his world wasn't filled with devices of this complexity. There were a few, but not many, and Johan had never seen one. At least not one that didn't fill a building. What made the sewing machine worse than the telephones or the lights was that it looked like he *should* be able to understand it. It wasn't all that different than a watermill, after all. Smaller, but there was a crank that turned and made other stuff happen.

Unfortunately, he wasn't allowed to remain in his state of confusion.

Instead, Brent Partow, one of young Master David's friends, saw his look and—as boys were wont to do—began to explain. Which would have been a great deal more helpful if the lad had spoken a comprehensible tongue. His English had the weirdest accent that Johan had ever heard, just like the rest of the up-timers, and it just got worse as the lad got into the details of the inner workings of the sewing machine. It wasn't the twang that bothered Johan. He had heard variations like that often enough. It was the technical words.

"It would seem a very complex piece of equipment," Johan offered. "It would probably take a long time to make. Perhaps something simpler?"

"We could, I guess. But it would be more likely to be copied," young Master David said. But Johan was an old soldier and an old bargainer, and he heard the lack of full confidence in David's voice. "Besides," David continued in a firmer voice, "the sewing machine is what we agreed on."

So it wasn't the best choice, just the one they could agree on. That was more than interesting. "Well, it looks very complicated to me."

"Looks are deceiving," Brent said. "It's not lots of different parts, so much as lots of the same few parts."

His twin brother, Trent, snorted at that. Frau Higgins said, "Never mind. What we're going to need you to do is help us talk to the local merchants and craftsmen so that we can have the parts made without telling them how to make the whole thing."

Higgins' Storage Lot
July 8, 1631

Johan walked his rounds along the small steel buildings that Lady Delia had called repurposed shipping containers and thought about the up-timers and the children and their project. He liked them, liked them a lot. They were kind to an old soldier who didn't deserve it, and they made him feel at home.

Johan had grown almost to manhood in Amsterdam, watching the best merchants and craftsmen on Earth go about their business. He knew that while the up-timers had great wealth, that wealth would be used up sooner or later unless they used it to build more. He understood that. He looked over at the chain link fence and shook his head. Like building a castle wall out of gold: you have to worry as much about someone stealing the fence as you do about them getting what's inside of it.

David and Donny's room, Higgins House
July 10, 1631

David sat at the desk and Johan on the bottom bunk. "No, the sewing machines are vitally important. And not just to us, to all of Grantville. We need to start producing goods, not just selling the stuff we brought with us."

Johan nodded. That seemed pretty obvious now that young Master David had pointed it out.

"If we can produce a sewing machine at a reasonable price, we can sell hundreds of them, or thousands."

Again, Johan nodded, but he wasn't entirely convinced this time. Still, it wasn't his place to be contradicting young Master David.

The young master continued to talk, and Johan continued to listen. He got the story of how they had decided on the sewing machine and how it wasn't nearly as complicated as it seemed. There were only a few parts that were beyond the abilities of the local smiths. How the lack of a bank loan had probably killed their plan to make sewing machines. "And I don't know what we're going to do."

Johan didn't either.

Delia Higgins' Sewing Room
July 12, 1631

Lady Delia waved Johan to the small couch, but Johan hesitated before he obeyed her. He knew she wasn't trying to trick him into showing a lack of respect for her station, but old habits died hard.

"I have a problem, Johan, and I think you might be able to help me with it. You've seen my doll collection." She waved at a shelf that went all the way around the sewing room, up near the ceiling. That shelf was packed with dolls, some in their boxes, but most in round plastic containers that David said were old three-liter soda bottles with their tops cut off and taped together. There had to be over a hundred dolls in this room alone, and Lady Delia had them in the living room and her bedroom as well. More of them in the living room. One wall of the living room was floor-to-ceiling shelves full of dolls.

"I think they are valuable in the here and now," Lady Delia continued, "and I want to sell them. But not at the Valuemart. I want to find a merchant who will buy them for resale in Hamburg, London or Vienna. Someplace like that." She looked at the dolls sadly, then her mouth tightened into firmness and she gave a sharp little nod.

Johan remembered his talks with David and the Partow twins about the sewing machine project and he guessed he knew what Lady Delia needed the money for. Well, Johan knew how to find merchants and how to deal with them. He had, on several occasions, been dog robber for this or that officer. He could bargain fairly well, especially when he was doing it for someone else.

Connie Myers' Home
July 12, 1631

Connie Myers sat beside her daughter and said, "Honey, you've got to stop doing this. Maybe go talk to somebody."

Darlene sniffed and wiped away the tears. "I'll be okay, Mom. I've got to get to work." Darlene jumped up from the couch and rushed out the front door to catch the bus out to the power plant.

Connie went back to the kitchen and made herself another cup of mint tea. Not that mint tea was a favorite; it was just what she could get right now.

"You know, Dink, we're lucky in a way," she said.

Her husband gave her a look.

"Well, we are," Connie insisted. "At least both our kids are with us. But poor Darlene has lost Jack and Johnny. She's devastated."

Thuringen Gardens
July 13, 1631

Johan was talking with some of the other survivors from the ill-fated attempt to take Badenburg. Unlike Johan, most of them had joined the

American army. They had spent the last fifteen minutes telling him how good life was in the American army with its shotguns.

Johan was having none of it. He leaned his chair against the wall, crossed his arms, and said, "Not me, boys, I'm too old for the army life. Besides, I have it better than you lot. Mrs. Higgins made me two new sets of clothes and bought me underwear with elastic." If he was in a place even a little less public he would have taken down his pants and shown them. He almost did anyway. He was proud of his new clothing. Instead, he focused on the clothing he could decently display. "And see my new shoes. I have another pair at home, and three pair of pants and four shirts. I've money for a pint when I want one, good food, and Mrs. Higgins has engaged to get me new teeth, at her expense, mind." Which she had.

Power Plant
July 14, 1631

"Darlene," said Bill Porter, Darlene's boss at the power plant, "This is Hans and this is Karl." He pointed at each young man as he spoke. "They will be working for you. Teach them how to read the dials so that you will have time to try and figure out how to build us some new dials."

Darlene looked up at the down-timers and didn't like them at all. Logically, she knew that the Ring of Fire wasn't their fault, but logic wasn't driving her emotional response. It was unfair that she should lose Jack and Johnny just so these down-time fucks could get an early introduction to twentieth-century tech. She looked at Bill, giving the down-timers barely a glance. "I have a lot to do, Bill. Maybe Leona?"

"Everyone has a lot to do, Darlene. Leona has her own set of down-timer assistants to train."

And that was that.

Darlene trained them and couldn't maintain her resentment, because they were as eager as puppies, and sharp. She learned that they were, or had been, students getting ready to study at the university at Jena on scholarship, but were fascinated by electricity. They were both, Darlene was sure, much smarter than she was. But she knew about gauges and what they did, even some of the theory. And she could read a technical manual written in English and grasp clearly what the technical terms meant, which they couldn't. Not yet.

Delia Higgins' Sewing Room
July 14, 1631

"Come in, Johan. Have a seat."

Johan came in and sat carefully on the little couch in Lady Delia's sewing room. She had her sewing chair turned away from the Singer. It was almost a hundred years old, but Johan knew that it was still up-time tech, which gave it a newness that contrasted with its age.

"We have a bunch of orders for storage space," Delia continued. "I've been being a greedy old fart, and it's time to stop." She shook her head. "I was just so scared right after the Ring of Fire. Our whole world gone. So I hid everything away and hoped no one would notice all I had and come take it."

That didn't seem greedy to Johan, just prudent.

"I could have left something in the storage containers that Grantville desperately needed, something that might have made the difference between life and death for all of us. Well, it stops now. We are going to open up all the containers where the renter was left up-time, and if there's something the emergency committee needs, we're going to give it to them. The rest, we'll sell at the Valuemart. That will free up the containers for renting, now that we have so many new people in town."

Higgins' Storage Lot
July 15, 1631

Johan slipped the bolt cutter over the lock and squeezed. The hard steel of the lock came loose. He pulled the lock out of the door and, with young Master David looking on, pulled open the door. In the storage container was a couch with cracked naugahyde upholstery. A backyard grill with butane tanks that Johan hoped were empty. This was the seventh storage container they'd opened so **far** and contained the third couch and the second backyard grill. There was also a chest of drawers with a cracked mirror.

"Why do people keep junk?" Master David muttered.

Johan looked at him, wondering if he was crazy. Well, not exactly. Master David often said similar things, and by now Johan was used to it. It wasn't exactly craziness. It was just that the up-timers were so rich. They threw everything away as a matter of course. The worst damaged thing in this container, probably the plastic bag full of broken toys, was worth a small fortune.

Young Master David must have seen his look because he held up his hands. "I know, Johan. 'I'm not asking about the here and now. But the people who put this stuff in the storage shed were doing it in the twentieth century, when this was junk. Those toys were made in China, and even new they were worth less than a month's rent of this container."

Johan considered what the young master was saying and understood it, mostly. The price of something depended a lot on when and where you were.

"Okay," David said. "Let's get it inventoried and off to the Valuemart."

Higgins' House
July 16, 1631

Johan ushered Federico Vespucci into the house. They'd met at the Valuemart while Johan was overseeing the delivery of yet another set of box springs for resale. He explained in Italian, "There are lots of things in the storage containers. More of the beds. Toys. Even some of the dolls like those." Johan pointed at the wall of dolls, and saw Vespucci's eyes go wide. Johan might as well have been pointing to shelves filled with gold and jewels.

"Not these, of course," Johan specified. "These are the private collection of Lady Delia Higgins and so not for sale." Johan sighed with all the pride and regret he could put into it, and Federico Vespucci looked at him, eyes narrowing.

"It's quite true," Johan insisted, and then made the introductions. He introduced Lady Delia, Mistress Ramona, and Masters David and Donny, giving them each their equivalent Italian title, with only a bit of rank inflation.

Johan translated as Mr. Vespucci explained that he was getting ready to return to Venice. He had arrived weeks after the Ring of Fire. Johan could tell that the merchant was desperate to be the first merchant to sell products from Grantville in Venice, no matter how he might try to hide it. Also that he wanted to buy quickly and be on his way.

Best of all, Vespucci did not speak English. The up-timers were wizards at any number of things, but bargaining, in Johan's view, was not among them.

Well, not *his* up-timers anyway. Johan was starting to take a somewhat proprietary view of Lady Delia, Mistress Ramona, and young Masters David and Donny. They knew a tremendous amount to be sure, but they weren't really, well, worldly. Which, he thought, made quite a bit of sense, since they weren't from his world, having come from a magical future.

Thus, they lacked the simple understanding that all merchants are thieves. It was purely certain that any merchant who had an opportunity to talk directly to them would rob them blind, talking them into selling their valuables for a pittance.

While it might not have been true of all up-timers, Johan was right about his up-timers. They rented their storage containers for a set monthly fee. Bought their groceries at the store where you either bought or didn't, but didn't haggle over the price. They hadn't even haggled much when buying their car. All in all, they had virtually no experience in the art of the haggle, and haggling is not one of those things you can learn from a book.

"The dolls are unique, with their posable limbs and inset hair, and are made of plastic, which cannot be duplicated, even in far-off China. Even to approximate them would be the work of a skilled artist working for months using ivory or the finest porcelain. See the lovely pink color? But, unfortunately, they are not for sale," Johan told Vespucci. "Now, about the furniture in the storage containers."

∞ ∞ ∞

Federico was no fool. He knew full well that the storage containers with their furniture, even the fancy comfortable mattresses, were little more than a come-on, a way to get him here to see the dolls. He knew that the scoundrel who had attached himself to these up-timers was a cad and a thief. That he was going to be robbed blind. Federico knew all that, and it didn't matter a bit.

Federico fought the good fight. He was a merchant after all, and a good one.

How did Johan know that plastic was so hard to make?

They brought out the encyclopedia and read him the passages about the industrial processes involved in making plastic. Which didn't matter, since the dolls were not for sale.

He would need proof that they were authentic up-time dolls.

They could provide certificates of authentication, proof that they not only came from Grantville, but from the personal collection of Delia Ruggles Higgins. Of course, the dolls weren't for sale.

All in all, with Johan's deliberate mistranslations and Delia's enthusiastic discussion of her dolls; it had the makings of a remarkably shrewd sales technique.

All of which wouldn't have worked at all, except Federico knew perfectly well what would happen when he reached Venice with the dolls. There would be a bidding war, and the dolls would be shipped to royal courts, wealthy merchants, and everything in between, from one end of the world to the other. All at exorbitant prices. Some, a very few, would actually end up as the prized toy of a very wealthy child. Most would end up in various collectors' collections of rare and valuable knickknacks.

It wasn't quite enough. Federico left that night with no commitments made.

July 16-18, 1631

That might have been the end of it. Not hardly. Johan would have found something. If nothing else, they would have offered a few more dolls. That was what Federico was expecting. Or failing that, Federico would have gone back and made the deal anyway. In spite of the urgent letters he had for delivery in Venice, he was not leaving Grantville without those dolls. But a deal under the current conditions would have meant bad blood. Real resentment, the kind of anger that means the person you're dealing with never wants to deal with you again, and warns their friends away. Says words like "thief" and "miser," not with a half-joking, half-respectful tone, but with real intent.

In any event, it wasn't necessary. Two weeks earlier, David had given Johan an old Playboy. It had happened at the end of a discussion of the fairer sex, in which young lad and old man had agreed that girls were complex and confusing, but sure nice to look at. He figured that the old guy would use it for the same thing he did. To read the articles, of course.

This was still the age when the quality of art was determined primarily by how closely it reflected reality. The photographs in a Playboy magazine looked quite real indeed, just somewhat, ah, more, than nature usually provides. This gave the pictures a certain amount of added artistic value. Johan noted this, and on the morning of the sixteenth, showed the Playboy to Master Vespucci, with the explanation that there were some forms of art that proper Christian ladies didn't appreciate. It was a deal closer. It saved everyone's pride. Several additional images were agreed on, and things were settled. Master Vespucci would get his dolls and get to keep his pride. Lady Higgins would be spoken of with respect, and even her scoundrel of a servant, as someone who knew how things worked.

The final deal was made. A consignment of selected dolls, all sizes and types, each with a signed and sealed certificate of authenticity, and undisclosed sundries, were exchanged for a rather large sum of money. In fact, most of the money that Master Vespucci had available to him in Thuringia. The things he'd been planning to buy in Badenburg would just have to find another buyer. The sundries were David's Playboys, all twenty-four of them. And fifty really raunchy color photos downloaded from the internet up-time, that he had used the last of his color ink to print.

Dentist's Office
July 20, 1631

"All right, Herr Kipper," Doctor Sims said. "Let's have a look. Open wide."

Johan opened his mouth and closed his eyes against the strange round light that surrounded the magnifying glass the doctor was using. The doctor used paddles to move Johan's tongue out of the way and to push against his teeth, then had him sit up. The walls were white and there were big pictures of teeth and gums on the wall.

"Here's the situation. You have a couple of cavities in the teeth you have left. I could fill those, but I don't have any partial plates that would fit your remaining teeth. What I can do is pull those last few and set you up with a full set. I have a couple of full sets that can be adjusted to fit you. I don't like pulling healthy teeth, and if I had access to the equipment and supplies needed to make partial plates. That's what I would recommend. But I don't have that access."

Johan didn't have to think about it long. He hated to lose the last of his teeth, but he knew they would be going anyway. He agreed.

Slowly, Johan Kipper was getting used to the up-timers, and at the same time he was coming to realize that he didn't agree with them about how the world worked. He liked what they thought, but to him David would always be young Master David. Mrs. Higgins, whatever she insisted on being called, was always going to be the mistress of the clan, as noble in his eyes as any queen in Christendom.

It was very nice that the up-timers thought down-timers their equals, but it wasn't true, not really.

Chapter 2—Bargainer in Chief

July 20, 1631
Delia Higgins' House

When Johan got back from the dentist's office, he had another surprise waiting for him.

"But, Lady Higgins, that's too much. Giving me any of the company is too much."

"Nonsense. And you need to stop calling me Lady Higgins. It's Mrs. Higgins or Delia."

"That wouldn't be proper, Lady Higgins. Chief Frost said you were a lady, and you own the lot and the dolls and the company. It would be above my place. And with all due deference, ma'am—" With an effort, Johan didn't call her Lady Higgins again. He wanted to avoid the distraction. "—there's no call, no call at all, for you to be giving a full twentieth part of the company to the likes of me. That's beyond my pay and maintenance. You up-timers, Lord love you, are too generous by half and half again."

Lady Higgins took a breath. "The sale of the dolls has been finalized, Johan, and you are the biggest part of the reason for that." She stuck a finger at him. "Don't you think I didn't notice what you were doing. Now the company is legally formed. And the kids insisted that I get sixty percent since the start-up capital came from my dolls. Brent, Trent, Sarah, and David each get ten percent, and they insisted I get the rest. But if it's mine, it's mine, and I can do with it what I want. I'm giving five percent to Ramona and five to Dalton and neither of them has done a thing to earn it. I'm giving two percent each to all the grandkids. I'm giving Jeff and Gretchen five percent as a belated wedding present. And I'm giving you five percent for your help in finding the buyer and negotiating the deal."

"What about your parents?" Johan asked. "Surely the . . ."

He trailed off as Delia shook her head. "After the way they've ragged on me over the whole project, they aren't getting any. Family is family, Johan, even if they are idiots. But business is business, and you are important to the business. I want you to have a reason to want it to succeed."

She wouldn't back down from that at all.

Well, Johan had a reason to want the business to succeed. A powerful reason. But it wasn't the stock, not exactly. It was that she had given him the stock and David Bartley had given him even more. David had given him himself.

There was one other reason for the gifts, and Johan got to watch as she explained it to the kids.

"I figure the thing most likely to kill the company is if you all give up on it, and the thing most likely to make that happen is if you feel you have lost control. That your decisions, your actions, don't matter. You know and I know that it's unlikely any of the others will ever vote their shares," Delia said. "Maybe Johan, but he'll probably vote the way David tells him to.'

"I remember the concern you all had that the grownups would take it away. Well, we won't. As of now, the four of you can outvote me, and nobody can outvote you without me on their side. This was your project in the beginning and it still is. I want that clear in your minds. You kids thought it up, you did the work, and more importantly, you'll still be doing the work. If it's going to work, you're the ones who'll make it work. If it's going to fail, well, that's you too.

"Delia grinned a very nasty grin. "Scary, ain't it?" She softened a bit. "I'll be here if you need advice. So will your parents. But this is yours."

Johan watched the faces of the youngsters as Lady Higgins said that. He could see how their expressions changed and firmed. Trust can be a heavy load, but it can strengthen even as it weighs you down.

July 23, 1631
Delia Higgins' House

Johan knocked on the sewing room door and then stepped into the room. "You wanted to see me, ma'am?"

Lady Higgins turned away from her sewing. "Yes. I talked to Judy Wendell earlier today, and she says we need to be spending more money. Do you think you can find me another guard or two?"

"I'm sure I can, ma'am, but where are we going to put them?" Johan considered. "I guess I could share the bedroom in the mobile, and if we hire more than one maybe we could clean out one of the storage containers."

"No, that won't work. Maybe I can move my sewing stuff into the living room and you can stay here?"

"I don't need this whole space, and I don't want to push you out of your work room." Johan had, in some ways, a better understanding of how much income was coming out of the sewing room than Delia did, **at** least in terms of relative value. The money Delia made from sewing paid for most of the groceries eaten by the family. Anything that interfered with that would be worse than the cost of hiring a couple of extra guards.

"You're sure?" Delia looked around. The room was full of stuff, baskets of clothing in need of repair. By now about half of it was clothing that had been originally made down-time. The Valuemart bought old

German clothing and sold it to Delia, then bought it back after she had fixed the tears and busted seams, and resold it. It was a fairly standard pattern for seventeenth-century Germany, even if Johan knew it seemed strange to up-timers.

July 24, 1631
Delia Higgins' House

"This is the life," Hans Bauer said.

Johan opened the refrigerator and pulled out a bottle of beer. It was down-time made, bottled in Grantville, and pasteurized. It was good quality beer, rich and dark with flavor. Johan used a bottle opener and passed over the bottle.

"It's sure better than catching a pike in Tilly's tercios," Johan agreed. "How are you liking life in the National Guard?"

"It's better than Tilly's tercios, but I envy you, Johan, I truly do."

"You don't have to, Hans. I talked to Lady Higgins, and I can get you a place here if you want." As he was speaking, Johan pulled a plastic, microwave-safe bowl out of the refrigerator and stuck it in the microwave. As was usual among up-time made stews, it was heavy on the meat. Delicious, but heavier on the meat than most down-timers were accustomed to.

While it warmed, he pulled a loaf of bread from the cupboard and sliced off a big piece. Bread machines were present in Grantville, and while they couldn't be reproduced down-time because they used integrated circuits, they could be repaired. The heating element, even the motors, could be rebuilt and strengthened. Bread machine bread was common in Grantville these days.

Johan stuck the bread in the microwave for a few seconds so it would be warm and passed it to Hans. Hans was a good fellow, sturdy and dependable, if not bright. He had some English, so he would at least be able to follow Master David's instructions, and he wasn't pockmarked like Johan was, so he wouldn't upset Mistress Ramona. He could be counted on to make his rounds on time every night and keep a good watch.

By the time the meal was done, Hans was Lady Higgins' second guard, and Johan went looking for a third. He also knew Dieter Eichel and Liesel Jung from Tilly's tercio. Liesel had a little English, though Dieter didn't have any. Dieter was okay, but Liesel was the real prize. Johan had decided that the Higgins family needed servants. It was indecent for people that wealthy not to have servants. It demeaned them even if they didn't understand it, and **it** made them seem miserly to the down-timers. Liesel would go to work, and by now Johan was familiar enough with Lady Higgins to know that she would start paying Liesel soon enough.

July 25, 1631
A Smithy in Badenburg

Johan watched quietly as young Master Brent went on, again, telling the blacksmith what the part did and why. "It's really just a lever," Brent said, "but it's clever how it works. This end rests against a rotating cam that makes one complete rotation every two stitches. The cam has a varying radius. As the cam rotates, the short end of the lever is moved in and out. That moves the long end of the lever up and down, pulling the thread or loosening it as needed to make the stitch. So it's very important that each end of the lever is the right length, and while the major stresses are vertical it needs enough depth to avoid bending. The model and the forms provide you with a system of measuring tools to tell how well the part fits within specifications." Then Brent looked at Johan to translate.

Johan did, sort of, in his way. "See the pattern drawn on the board with the nails in it?" The board was a piece of one-by-eight about a foot long that Brent and Trent had made. He waited for the nod. Then took the wooden model and placed it on the nails where it fell easily to cover the internal line and leave the external line exposed. He wiggled it. The inside line remained hidden. The outside line remained in view, as there wasn't much wiggle room.

"See the way it covers the inside line and doesn't cover the outside line? This model would pass the first test if it was iron."

He removed the model from the nails and slid it through a slot in the wood. "It's thin enough it would pass the second test." He then tried to slip it through another slot but it wouldn't go. "It's thick enough it would pass the third test. The fourth test is a weight test. But if it's good iron and it passes these, it should pass the last as well. So that's the deal. Each one of these that passes the tests, we'll pay you. If it doesn't pass, we don't buy it."

Then the bargaining began in earnest. It took a while, but Johan got a good price. Not quite so good as he wanted, but better than he really expected. With the craftsman's warning, "Mind, all my other work will come first."

And so it went. Over the following days, they visited craft shops of several sorts. They ordered finished parts where they could, and blanks where the techniques of the early seventeenth century weren't up to the task. The blanks would be finished by the machines they had designed.

August 12, 1631
Delia Higgins' House

Johan was cleaning his pistol when Liesel knocked on the door. "Mrs. Higgins wants you in the living room. Some townsman wants to talk about the sewing machines … "

He looked at the clock. It was two thirty in the afternoon, and he'd been out with Master David and Brent talking to a leather worker in Saalfeld till noon. He had an appointment with a smith in Rudolstadt in another hour, but this probably took precedence. He quickly reassembled the six-shot revolver that they had found in one of the storage sheds, and put on his pistol belt and the baseball cap.

∞ ∞ ∞

Johan entered the living room.

"Johan, this is Herr Schmidt," Delia said. The room had fewer dolls now. It gave the doll shelves a half-empty feeling, at least to Johan.

Then Delia said, "He's here to discuss the sewing machine business. At least, I think that's why he's here. Between my lack of German and his lack of English, I'm not entirely sure."

Johan gave the man a nod. He thought he recognized him through his resemblance to his son. He thought for a minute . . . Adolf Schmidt? No, that was the son. Karl . . . that was it. "Herr Schmidt, I think we talked to your son Adolph."

"Yes. Adolph said you insisted on a surcharge if we weren't willing to take American dollars."

"Yes, I am afraid so. The bank of Grantville is hesitant to accept the local silver coins. And carrying large sums of silver to Badenburg is a risk, if a small one. We find it much easier to simply write a check."

"A check?"

Johan reached into his right breast pocket and pulled out his checkbook. He had a bank account now at the First National Bank of Grantville.

Lady Higgins gestured them to the dining table and they all sat.

He showed Herr Schmidt the check book. "Right here, where it says 'pay to the order of,' we would fill in your name or the name of your company account. I really recommend that you get an account at the Grantville bank or the credit union, Herr Schmidt. That way you can turn over the check and have the money transferred to your account in perfect safety."

Johan watched Herr Schmidt's face and was amused. Not for the first time, either. He knew precisely what was going through the mind of the Badenburg foundry owner. How was Schmidt to know if they had the money in their account to pay the check? Considering that Schmidt was from Badenburg and not living in Grantville, he was probably also wondering if he could trust the bank.

"You can find out if a check is good readily enough. A simple phone call." He stopped. There was no phone service to Badenburg yet, though they were putting up the phone lines for it now. Even so, it would only be the one hook up for the whole town. It was going to be a while before Badenburg had full phone service. It hadn't been a slip of the tongue. It had been a reminder that in Grantville you could call the bank or the police readily.

They talked about money, but both Johan and Lady Higgins insisted that they couldn't do anything final till they talked to Master David. Johan could tell that Schmidt thought it was a ploy, and Johan was willing enough that he think that. He saw no reason not to use the fact that Master David needed to sign off on any agreements as a bit of extra pressure on Karl Schmidt. But it wasn't just a ploy. Young Master David was showing signs of turning into a real man of business.

Johan watched them as he translated, each for the other. Herr Schmidt and Lady Higgins were alike in some ways and different in others. He didn't think Lady Higgins really trusted Herr Schmidt, which Johan felt was a good thing. The up-timers, especially his up-timers, tended to be too trusting.

Bank of Grantville
August 15, 1631

Karl Schmidt sat on a chair in the loan officer's cubicle, and Lady Higgins sat on another. Johan stood in a corner of the small space and watched as Herr Schmidt and Lady Higgins each signed the contracts. Master David and Miss Sarah had convinced Herr Schmidt to open a business account at the Bank of Grantville, which was useful not just for the foundry's dealings with HSMC but its dealings with all the other shops in town.

There were two contracts, one in English and the other in German, but both had been checked and they were consistent. Once Lady Higgins and Herr Schmidt had signed, the bank officer signed as witness and pulled out the notary stamp. He shook Lady Delia's hand and Herr Schmidt's.

Karl would be having several new devices made for his foundry, using in part money from the contract with HSMC, and having an account at the Bank of Grantville meant that he could buy a device from Olly Reardon with a check. And Olly could verify the check with a phone call.

It meant that even money spent in Badenburg was staying in Grantville.

September 10, 1631
Delia Higgins' House

Johan opened the door for Karl Schmidt and his family. This evening Johan was wearing a dress coat with sergeant's stripes on the sleeve. He was the Higgins' Guard Sergeant, and this was fancy dress. He showed Herr Schmidt, his son Adolph, and his three daughters into the living room where Lady Higgins and Mistress Ramona were waiting.

Ramona had invited Karl Schmidt and his family. They had been seeing each other since mid-August. Not every day, but once a week or so, Karl would bring in a load of parts and Ramona would take the afternoon off.

In the beginning, Master David and Lady Higgins had been concerned about the developing relationship between Karl and Ramona. But David wasn't, not anymore.

Acculturation works both ways, and it works faster on kids. Johan had been acculturating David right along. David had had a conversation with Master Schmidt. Ramona Higgins was a lady of high station, with a family which would take it very badly if she were treated with a lack of respect. Normally such comments from a boy just turned fifteen might be ignored. In this case, however, Johan was sitting a few feet away cleaning a double-barreled shotgun and adding translation and mistranslation as needed. Besides, in the discussions about the sewing machine parts, David had gotten to know Karl a little bit. He was bigoted, but no more than most, and he wasn't a user, unlike some of David's mom's previous men.

Chapter 3 — Moving Up in the World

October 11, 1631
Delia Higgins' Garage

Master David and Johan got off the bus about a block and a half away from the Higgins house, and it wasn't until they were turning into the driveway that they realized there was anything going on. There were too many cars in the parking lot.

Usually there were one or two vehicles, most often a truck, sometimes a push cart or a horse-drawn wagon, here to pick something up or put something in the containers. Today, there were five cars and three wagons in the parking lot.

While Master David went in to see what was going on, Johan went to the storage lot office.

"What's happening with all the cars?" Johan asked even before he closed the door of the mobile home.

"Close the door," said Dieter. "Don't you know we're in the middle of the Little Ice Age?"

Johan was already closing the door. The day was cold, even for an old mercenary who was wearing the best clothing he had ever owned.

"Brent and Trent got the sewing machine working," Liesel said. "And people have been showing up all afternoon. Karl Schmidt brought the whole family. Mr. Marcantonio is here. So are a couple of people from the Grantville bank and the credit union. The Wendells are here, and the Partows."

"I don't see what all the excitement is about," Hans complained. "It's a machine that sews. The up-timers have all sorts of machines that do all sorts of things. Mrs. Higgins already has a machine that sews. She used it to sew the patches on my coat." Hans pointed at his coat to prove the point.

Johan didn't try to explain it to him.

Dieter said, "Say, Johan, could you loan me a thousand dollars? I'd like to buy a horse to get around on." He was grinning, but the question was at least half serious. They all knew that Johan owned five percent of the Higgins Sewing Machine Company.

"Huh?" Hans asked. They also knew that Johan was getting precisely the same pay that they were, not even extra for being the guard sergeant.

"That share he has in the sewing machine company," Liesel explained carefully. Hans could get angry if you challenged his intelligence too blatantly. "Now that the sewing machine company is making sewing machines, it's worth more. I heard people talking about it over at the house."

"Yes, but he can't sell it, can he?" Hans asked. "Not when Lady Higgins gave it to him. That would be . . . bad."

"Yes, it would be," Johan agreed. "Dieter is just going to have to save up and buy his own horse."

"Dieter isn't getting a horse until I have a sewing machine," Liesel said, and both Johan and Hans laughed.

"Hans, with all these people here I want you to take an extra round through the storage lot, in case someone got lost."

Hans nodded and went to the rack by the door. He grabbed a scarf and a fur cap, then put them and a great coat on. When he went out, he let in another blast of frigid air.

Once he was gone, Liesel told Dieter severely, "Don't confuse him."

"Wasn't trying to confuse Hans, sweetheart," Dieter said placatingly. "I was teasing Sergeant Moneybags here."

"What makes you think I'm so rich all of a sudden?" Johan asked.

"It's all they're talking about over there," Liesel said. "How the Higgins Sewing Machine Company is worth ten times what it was yesterday."

"That, and that you conned your way into the affections of a little old lady. Took advantage of her and a bunch of kids," Dieter added.

Dieter held up his hands when Johan turned to him. "I'm not saying it. Some of the up-timers up at the house are saying it."

Johan bit back his response. Something about the close family inbreeding of anyone who thought that. He took a breath and asked, "What are they saying, Liesel?"

"Everything they can think of." Liesel sniffed. "That Master David and Miss Sarah and the Partow twins are all too young to be running a company that may turn out to be vital to the welfare of Grantville. That you have been manipulating Lady Higgins." Liesel hesitated then said in a rush, "They can't figure out how you're doing it the way you look, but you used your wiles on her the same way you suckered Vespucci. That the fact that Lady Higgins gave you five percent of the company is proof."

"I knew that was a bad idea, but Lady Higgins insisted. Mostly because she was angry with her parents."

"Why didn't she just keep it, then?" Dieter asked, sounding truly curious.

Johan leaned back in his chair, rubbing his temples. The truth was he didn't know why Lady Higgins gave him part of the company, even though she told him. "She said it was to give me a stake in the success of the company."

"That makes sense," Liesel said.

"Not to me," Johan said. "I have my own reasons for taking care of Master David and the whole family." He remembered that day when David Bartley looked him in the eye. "I am not afraid of you," Master David had said, and he meant every word. "I don't have to trap you into doing something that would be an excuse to punish you. I don't need to make you weak to feel strong, or safe. That's why we act the way we do, Johan! The way that seems so wrong to you. Because we are not afraid. Not the way these German lords are. And because we are not afraid of you, you don't have to be afraid of us." Master David had proved that since then, proved it every day since that first day. Johan Kipper had felt small and mean every day of his life. Until the day he met Master David, but Master David had never made him feel small, not once. Other up-timers had sometimes. But never Master David and never Lady Higgins.

October 26, 1631
Higgins' House

Delia Higgins tapped her coffee cup with her spoon three times. "The first stockholders meeting of the Higgins Sewing Machine Corporation is hereby called to order. Is anyone recording this auspicious occasion for posterity?"

"I am, Mrs. Higgins," Sarah Wendell said, holding up her dad's digital camera.

"Me, too," said Trent Partow, holding up a cassette tape recorder.

"I was afraid of that," Lady Higgins said, and Johan struggled not to laugh. He wasn't the only one. David Marcantonio was grinning and Dalton Higgins was smiling. Mistress Ramona was too, although as usual she was looking a little confused. Liesel was in the kitchen and Johan was standing by in case anyone needed anything.

"Okay. First we have some real business. It has been proposed to sell David Marcantonio two thousand shares of Higgins Sewing Machine

Corporation common stock to clear the debt for the last two machines we bought from him. Do any stockholders have any objections to that?" Lady Higgins looked around the table. Her eyes seemed to rest on Dalton a little longer than on anyone else, but he didn't object.

"Good, then. Without dissent. Sarah, go ahead."

Dave Marcantonio handed Sarah a check for two thousand dollars and Sarah handed him a stock certificate in exchange.

Then Sarah pulled out the bill for the last two production machines and handed the bill and the check to Mr. Marcantonio. He tore up the check, marked the bill paid in full, and handed it back.

"There, Dave," Lady Higgins said. "You're now officially a stockholder, and as such you can be on the board of directors. I nominate you to the board of directors. In fact, I nominate you to the post of Chairman of the Board."

"Forget it, Delia. I'll sit on the board, but you ain't sticking me with the chairmanship."

"I nominate Delia Higgins to the post of Chairwoman of the Board," Sarah said.

"I second the nomination," Dave Marcantonio said.

"I move the nominations be closed," Trent Partow added.

"It's been moved that nominations for Chairman of the Board be closed. Any objections?"

For just a moment, Johan thought Dalton Higgins was going to object, but he didn't.

"Very well. We will vote by a show of hands. All those for David Marcantonio?" Lady Higgins raised her hand even as she said it. But her hand was the only one to come up.

"Thirty thousand votes for David Marcantonio. All for Delia Higgins?"

Master David raised his hand. So did Sarah, Trent, Brent, and Dave Marcantonio. Master David looked at Johan and rolled his eyes up. Johan got the signal and raised his hand, feeling a bit weird even as he did it. Then Dalton and Ramona Higgins raised their hands. Johan counted it up in his head. Master David twelve thousand shares, Sarah, Trent and Brent ten thousand each, made forty-two thousand. Johan's five thousand and Mr. Marcantonio's two thousand made it forty-nine thousand, Mistress Ramona's five thousand and her proxy for Master Donny's two made it fifty-six thousand. Dalton's five made sixty-one and the six thousand shares he was voting for his kids made sixty-seven thousand votes for Lady Higgins.

Lady Higgins looked around at the raised hands and the girls and said, "Oh, all right. But I nominate Dave Marcantonio to the board of the Higgins Sewing Machine Corporation. Any objections?"

There was silence.

"Let the minutes show that Mr. Marcantonio was elected by acclamation of the shareholders present."

Master David held up a finger.

"Yes, David?"

"I would like to nominate Johan Kipper to the board."

"What?" It came out without Johan willing it. Master David hadn't mentioned this to him. No one had mentioned this to him.

"I second the nomination," Sarah said. "I'm a stockholder and the bylaws give me that right."

"I third the nomination," said Brent Partow.

"You can't third a nomination," Sarah said.

"I just did, didn't I?" Brent said.

Lady Higgins tapped her coffee cup with the spoon again, and silence returned to the room. "Johan Kipper has been nominated and seconded to the board of the Higgins Sewing Machine Corporation. All stockholders in favor, please raise your hands."

Master David, Miss Sarah, Trent and Brent all raised their hands immediately, then so did Lady Higgins and Dave Marcantonio. That only left Mistress Ramona who was voting her shares and Master Donny's, and Dalton who was voting his shares and those of his children Mindy, Milton, and Mark. Dalton didn't raise his hand, but after another moment Mistress Ramona did.

"With a vote of eighty-one thousand shares," Lady Higgins said, "Johan Kipper is elected to the board of directors of the Higgins Sewing Machine Corporation. Sit down, Director Kipper. It's inappropriate for a member of the board to stand around like he's waiting to serve the soup. And stop calling me Lady Higgins. You're a member of the board yourself now."

Johan just stood there. Liesel poked him in the ribs and he hesitantly went to the dining table and sat down. Finally, he found his voice. "Chief Frost told me you were a lady, and I have seen no reason to doubt it."

"Hear, hear," said Dave Marcantonio then he got a twinkle in his eye. "In fact, I propose that the official address for the chairperson of the board of the Higgins Sewing Machine Corporation be lady or lord, as fits their gender. Do I hear a second?"

"I second the motion," Brent Partow said.

Even as Delia Higgins said, "You're out of order, Dave. Not to mention out of your ever-loving mind."

"Motion has been made and seconded," Dave said. "This is a stockholder meeting, Delia, not a board meeting. Any stockholder can make a motion."

"You still have to be recognized by the chair and I am the chair."

Master David held up that finger again.

"Yes, David?"

"I move that the chairperson of the board be addressed as lady or lord as appropriate to their gender."

"I second," Dave Marcantonio said.

"I third," Brent said.

Lady Higgins looked at Master David, and said. "I don't recognize you." Then she looked around the room. "I never saw that kid before in my life."

"Mother," Mistress Ramona said, shocked.

"Oh, good grief," said Dalton.

Delia looked at her son. "You shouldn't take this stuff too seriously, Dalton."

"I don't know why we're bothering with it at all," Dalton said. "Fine, David and his friends have got their company up and running, sort of. They are turning out treadle-powered sewing machines, sort of." He sighed. "Look, Mom, I appreciate the gesture, but I have to get back to work." He stood up. "Tell you what, Mom. I'm giving you my proxy. Feel free to vote my stock and the kids' stock as you see fit." Then he left.

The gesture that Dalton Higgins was talking about was the gift of five thousand shares of HSMC stock to him and two thousand each to his three children. Johan knew that he also had five thousand shares of HSMC. But, unlike Johan, Dalton hadn't been involved in the design and production of the sewing machines. He wasn't all that close to his mother and had been busy with his job and his family. Besides which, Dalton Higgins was an up-timer. He didn't understand what sewing machines meant, not like down-timers did.

∞ ∞ ∞

As they were leaving the house, Johan said, "You shouldn't have done that, Master David."

"We trust you, Johan," Master David said. "We need someone we trust on the board, Director Kipper."

"It's not that we don't trust Mrs. Higgins or Mr. Marcantonio," Sarah Wendell was quick to point out. "But you're out in the field with us, working with the down-timer suppliers."

"Forget that," Brent Partow said. "We need someone we can trust in the board meetings. Someone who isn't going to override us—" He made little quote gestures with his fingers. "—'for our own good.' "

November 2, 1631
Thuringian Gardens

The seven girls trooped in, carrying bags. Johan watched as they set their bags on the table. Johan knew Judy the Younger Wendell and had seen several of the rest now and again since he'd been working for the Higgins family. Judy was Sarah Wendell's little sister and the rest were her friends.

"This is Herr Gerber. He is from the Netherlands," Johan said, "And this is Monsieur Carloni from Genoa. Fraulein Wendell, would you introduce your friends?"

Judy did, going from the oldest, Susan Logsden, to the youngest, Hayley Fortney. There was a solemn, almost tragic, air about the girls as they removed the dolls from the bags. They introduced the dolls, mentioning character traits. Like the imagined fact that one Barbie liked strawberry ice cream and another blueberry waffles. The dolls were, with a few exceptions, not in very bad shape, though it was obvious that they were dolls that had been played with, not collector's dolls still in the box. In other circumstances, that might have made them less valuable. There were only a very limited number of up-timer dolls in the world. Add to that the cachet that anything owned by an up-timer had, and they were worth their weight in gold. More than that. In these circumstances, the fact that they were actually played with by real up-timer little girls made them more, not less, valuable. Provenance was important here, and the computer printouts that came out of the bags next proved that Judy and her friends knew that.

When Haley Fortney started saying that maybe she should keep her construction worker Barbie, the price almost doubled.

They kept some of the money they got for the dolls, a bit over a thousand American dollars, split among the seven girls. But they bought eight thousand, two hundred fifty-four shares of HSMC at the price of one dollar a share.

Those, thankfully, were the last shares sold at the initial offering price, and that because Judy had gotten an agreement on the price before the corporate papers had been filed. From now on, the price would be determined by the market. And the Grantville Exchange currently had the price at $1.57 per share.

November 14, 1631
Mobile Home, Higgins Storage Lot

"Hey, Johan." Dieter waved as Johan came through the gate. "Liesel says that HSMC passed five dollars a share?"

"News must have gotten out about the Grantville bank agreeing to buy our loans."

"Would you mind explaining that?" Dieter asked, as he got to the stairs to the mobile home.

"It means we can sell a sewing machine on credit, or a rent with an option to buy deal, and the bank will loan us money based on the loans we made to the buyer. We still have to pay the money back, but it means we have, or can get, cash to buy parts and generally run the business. Miss Sarah and that old crank at the bank were going round and round on how much interest we were going to be charged. She finally had to threaten to take our business to Uriel Abrabanel."

"What does that mean?" Liesel asked, as they stepped into the mobile home.

Mistress Ramona was looking confused and Johan thought the question was at least half for her benefit.

"It means that we can sell the sewing machines as fast as we make them."

Ramona was looking worried and, surprisingly, Liesel was too. Liesel mouthed "Later," with a glance at Ramona.

November 14, 1631
Higgins House

Johan stepped into the kitchen and looked around. No one else was here. "What's bothering you, Liesel?"

Liesel turned away from the stove. She was fixing stuffed potatoes for lunch. They were one of the recipes developed by the cooking show on Grantville TV. They were stuffed with shredded cabbage, just enough ground pork for flavor, and local goat cheese, with a bit of sage, chives, and a little minced turnip, all broiled to a brown crispness. They were one of Johan's favorite foods.

"I was talking to Margaret, who knows Mary Gerber, who is walking out with Peter Strauss, who works in the Schmidt foundry. And she says that Peter says that Karl Schmidt is getting ready to go into competition with HSMC."

Johan took a couple of steps, then sat down at the kitchen table. It wasn't really all that much of a surprise. If it hadn't been Karl Schmidt, it would have been someone else. The problem was that it would mean losing the Schmidt foundry as a supplier, and the Schmidt foundry was selling them quite a few vital parts at prices that none of the smithies in the area could match. "That will be a problem, but I don't think he can match our price."

"It's not that. It's Mistress Ramona," Liesel said. "Whoever wins, she's going to get caught in the middle between her Karl and Master David."

"Oh," Johan admitted. "I hadn't considered that."

"You can't tell David," Liesel said.

"Well, I have to tell someone," Johan said. "It's a threat to the company."

∞ ∞ ∞

He ended up telling Lady Higgins about the rumored threat to the company, and she too insisted they not tell Master David.

"Don't borrow trouble, Johan," Delia Higgins said flatly. "And don't start a pissing match between David and Karl Schmidt. Let me handle it."

December 12, 1631
Higgins' House

Johan opened the door for Karl Schmidt and his family. He might be a director of the Higgins Sewing Machine Company now, but he still took his position in the Higgins household seriously. The rest of the Sewing Circle, as David, Brent, Trent and Sarah were being called, were already here.

Liesel and Dieter took the Schmidt girls' cloaks and Karl's and Adolph's coats. It was December in the Little Ice Age. It wasn't warm. But the central heat was running, and the house was toasty warm inside.

Johan knew what was going on and had agreed not to let David in on the negotiations. David was a good lad, but he still had a great deal of up-timer romanticism, especially where his mother was concerned. Johan knew what was going on, because he was deeply involved in the negotiations. Lady Higgins was as pragmatic about such things as a lady had to be.

Karl was going to ask to marry Ramona tonight, and Johan was worried. He understood how things were done in the seventeenth century. Karl expected a considerable dowry, but had also offered a major dower. A family merger that would make both families stronger. Marrying for money or connections wasn't considered crude or mercenary. It was the standard practice, and marrying without proper attention paid to such concerns was flighty and foolish.

Officially, they were here to celebrate the sale of the fiftieth sewing machine, which had happened the previous week. They were making a profit on the sewing machines now, but not enough of one. It would take them years at this rate just for the investments Lady Higgins had made to be paid back.

Once they were seated, and before dinner was served, Karl said, "I would like to talk to you all about a proposal I have. I have already spoken of it to Ramona and Madam Higgins, but without your agreement they will not agree."

Karl hesitated, then . . . "I wish to take over the Higgins Sewing Machine Corporation. I will put in my foundry to pay for fifty thousand shares of stock. I wish to wed Ramona, and with the wedding I will control her stock. Together with Mrs. Higgins, I would control over fifty percent of the outstanding stock. If you all agree, she has agreed to give me her support."

"Hear me out," Karl demanded, apparently unaware that no one was in any hurry to interrupt. "You four have done a tremendous thing. Four children have started a company that may someday be worth more than some kingdoms. You have brought wealth into the world, but starting a company is not the same thing as running it. Already there are others interested in producing sewing machines. So there will be competition and alternatives.

"Even if you do everything right, you will be at a disadvantage because people will not want to deal with children if they can deal with an adult. Others will find it easier to buy iron and other materials. People will say 'Do you want to trust a sewing machine that was made by children having a lark? Or would you rather have one made by mature men of consequence?' Besides, you have schooling yet to complete, so you will not be able to pay the company the attention it needs."

Karl talked on. He talked about potential problems, he talked about what he would like to do, how he wanted to make the company grow. Johan listened with less than half an ear. He'd heard it before. The important voice here would be Master David's.

David looked at Mistress Ramona to find her looking at him. Her eyes begged him not to kill this. She was almost in tears, afraid of what he would do. He looked at Lady Higgins as she caught his eye, looked at Ramona, then at Karl, and nodded. He looked to Sarah. She saw him looking at her and gave a slight shrug. And Johan watched it all.

Masters Brent and Trent were looking rebellious and betrayed. Johan watched David catch their eyes and mouth the word "wait." David turned his attention back to Karl, and the business part of the proposal.

It was fair. Johan knew that. The foundry was worth more than twenty-five percent of the company when you included Karl's connections with suppliers and customers, and both would increase in worth with the merger.

David looked at Adolph, and Johan followed his glance to see Adolph looking like he had a mouth full of sauerkraut. Johan knew that Adolph did not approve.

Karl was running down now.

Lady Higgins said, "Perhaps we should give the kids a chance to talk it over? Why don't you four go out in the garden and talk it out?"

The kids headed for the garden.

∞ ∞ ∞

The kids talked it out. Brent and Trent wanted to say no at first. It wasn't that they found the prospect of running a sewing machine company all that exciting. It wasn't.

"Oh, I don't know," said Trent, "I just hate the idea of losing."

"What makes you think you're losing?" David asked. "You're gonna be rich, and Karl's gonna do most of the work to make you that way. You never wanted to be the CEO anyway."

"What about you?" Brent asked. "You did want to be the CEO. Don't try to deny it. We were gonna be the chief engineers, Sarah was the chief financial officer and you were gonna be the CEO. The wheeler-dealer. So how come?"

David looked at the ground. He moved a rock with his toe. Then he said quietly, "Mom. She loves the guy and I think he loves her in his way. He'll treat her right."

Then, because mush is not an appropriate emotional state for a fifteen-year-old boy or a captain of industry, "Besides, it's a good deal. The foundry will really increase production once it's upgraded a bit."

∞ ∞ ∞

Sarah didn't buy the last part for a moment. Oh, it was true enough, but it wasn't what had decided David, and she knew it. David was doing it for his mother. She wouldn't have fought it after that, even if she had cared, but the truth was she didn't much care. She was more concerned now with other things.

December 25, 1631
Myers Home

Darlene Myers watched, unable to touch, as Jack struggled to make Christmas for little Johnny without her. They had gotten her insurance money, but without her income and with the extra spent on babysitting, finances were tight. Then little Johnny insisted, "I want Mommy!" and Jack said, "Mommy's gone away."

A part of Darlene remembered—even in her sleep—that she had been having this dream at least once a week since the Ring of Fire. Not Christmas day, but whatever day it was. She tried to wake up, but the dream rolled on.

They opened their presents and had Christmas dinner and then the wave front hit. It wasn't instant. There was plenty of time for Jack to feel the fabric of space time ripped apart by the wave front of changing time, for little Johnny to cry for a mommy whose transfer in time was the cause of the wave front of changing time that was ripping apart the very atoms that made him.

Darlene jerked up in her bed, with her shout of terror dying into sobs.

January 17, 1632
Power Plant

Darlene entered the power plant machine shop. "What's on for today?" She'd had the dream again last night, but little Johnny hadn't called for Mommy. He was forgetting her. Jack would be dating again, meeting other women. Johnny needed a mother.

She forced her mind back to the present. Her job now was to read technical manuals and answer down-timer questions about capacitance and other up-timer concepts that don't translate well into seventeenth-century German.

Darlene was trying to be upbeat, she really was. She made more money than she had up-time, but not knowing if Jack and Johnny still existed, if they were living their lives in ignorance of the disaster, the changes Grantville wrought on the universe would cause. Or if they had already been wiped away to exist only in her memory. The common belief that there were now two branches of time, that the universe of her birth was proceeding on, undisturbed by the Ring of Fire . . . It seemed to Darlene Myers that that was just wishful thinking. The laws of thermodynamics seemed to make such an outcome impossible.

Yes, the Ring of Fire was doing great things for the down-timers. But what about the up-timers they had left behind?

April 10, 1632
Wendell House

Sarah Wendell was still muttering. "You really should have done this a month ago."

Johan didn't sigh. For one thing, she was right, and he knew she was right. Which didn't make not sighing easier, just more necessary.

Before the Ring of Fire, the bread and butter of the Wendell household had been the preparation of taxes. Now, with Mr. and Mrs. Wendell working for the Finance Subcommittee, Sarah, with help from several of her classmates, had effectively taken over. And she had been harping on the need to get the taxes done sooner rather than later.

Johan Kipper was a taxpayer. After a lot of shouting in the Emergency Committee, and the run-up to elections, citizens and legal residents of the New United States paid income tax. For the mine workers and the power plant workers, it worked almost exactly like it had worked before the Ring of Fire, and to a large extent the same was true for anyone who had a job or ran a business. Mistress Ramona Higgins, for instance, was still an employee of the Higgins Storage Facility and Lady Higgins withheld taxes from her salary every month. For Johan, Hans, Dieter and Liesel, Mrs. Higgins withheld taxes based on their salary, but had not withheld for their maintenance—which was, it turned out, taxable income.

"You would have saved a bunch of worry."

Since the incorporation of HSMC, and Johan's appointment to the board, he had received a salary, most of which had stayed in the bank. What really worried him was the effect the merger had had on the price of his stock. When HSMC incorporated, they set the value of the stock at one dollar a share. After the merger between HSMC and the Schmidt foundry in December of 1631, the price of the stock had gone from $9.56 to $41.32 in eight days. It had dropped a little after the first of the year, but it was still over two hundred thousand dollars worth of stock.

"Capital gains aren't taxed till they're realized," Sarah continued.

"What?"

"You don't have to pay taxes on your stock until you sell it." Sarah looked annoyed. "You ought to know that."

Johan didn't know why he should know that. The intricacies of up-timer tax law . . . Well, they weren't any worse than the complex of German taxes and tithes, but they were different. And an old soldier, like Johan was, didn't have much to do with taxes anyway.

"You have to pay taxes on dividend income. So that wedding dividend that Karl Schmidt is talking about will be taxable, but that won't be till next year. No, the only real trouble you're going to have is with the maintenance Mrs. Higgins provided. That's taxable income."

"I know that," Johan said. "I have plenty in the bank to cover that."

"You won't have to. Mrs. Higgins is paying a maintenance bonus to cover the taxes on maintenance. And this year, she's doing the withholding, so it won't be an issue next year.

"If you had just come to me around the first of the year. You would have saved yourself a bunch of worry and I wouldn't be doing this when I'm swamped with the taxes of half of Grantville."

"Sorry, Miss Sarah. There has been a lot to do." That was perfectly true since the merger.

"Even if you get a loan against your stock, you won't pay taxes until you sell the stock to pay off the loan."

"Really? What would I get a loan for?" Johan asked.

"To invest," Sarah said. "HSMC isn't the only new company in Grantville. You need a diversified portfolio. I'm managing David's. And the twins' and Mrs. Higgins' portfolios, to make sure that we don't have all our eggs in one basket. And with the merger with Karl Schmidt's foundry, we can get an excellent interest rate from the credit union if we use our stock as collateral. There is a lot of real property involved in that."

Johan, by now, mostly understood what she was saying. On the other hand, he didn't know all that much about what was happening in the Grantville stock market. Not enough to trust himself to pick the right stocks. "You're handling it for Master David?"

"Yes, and Trent and Brent. David's busy running around for Herr Schmidt, and Trent and Brent don't care about anything but their gizmos."

"Would you handle mine too?" Johan said, now realizing why Master David insisted that he come over here.

"Sure," Sarah said, smiling. "It gives me a bigger pot of money to work with." She pulled out a document. "Look this over, and talk it over with David and Mrs. Higgins. Then, if you're sure, sign it and bring it back."

Johan took the document and read it through. It wasn't that long. It was a limited power of attorney authorizing Sarah Wendell to use his stock as collateral for loans and to invest the money, along with any other money he gave her. There was a clause that relieved her of liability if the investments lost money, but even that was fairly straightforward. Johan had been looking over similar documents ever since he got put on the board. "I'll sign it now," he said. "It's not the form, it's you I trust, Miss Sarah." He signed the document and wrote her a check for the better part of what he had in the bank.

Chapter 4—Weddings and Plan

April 22, 1632
Mobile Home, Higgins Storage Lot

"Did he ask her out?" Liesel asked.

"Yes, this morning." Johan laughed. "Very worried he was about it too. Once he remembered he isn't allowed to date. Lady Higgins was about to burst out laughing over it."

"I think it's cute," Liesel said.

"I think it's a problem waiting to happen," Dieter said. "None of these up-timers know how to handle their money. If they didn't make it by waving their hands and printing more dollars, they would all be paupers by now."

"American dollars are good money," Johan insisted. Much more than Dieter and Liesel, he'd been involved—at least peripherally—in the discussions of Grantville money.

"Did I say it wasn't?" Dieter asked. "I'm happy enough to get American dollars. They're better than *Kipper und Wipper* money, that's for sure. All I'm saying is, they don't know how to handle it. And David, little Donny, maybe even Lady Higgins, are all going to marry for love. Then where will we be? They need to be practical about this now that they are rich. You know, Lady Higgins gave all that money to the school concrete program? Well, she borrowed it from the bank. It's part of—"

"Enough, Dieter," Liesel said. "I swear, you'd worry if they gave you a million dollars."

"Well, of course," Dieter said, grinning now. "I don't have any idea what to do with a million dollars. What about you, Mr. Director Kipper? You're a good fifth of the way there."

"Never mind that," Liesel insisted. "I want to hear what David's going to do."

"He's on the phone in the big house," Johan said, "calling to invite the whole Wendell family to the opening of *The Importance of Being Earnest*. That way it's not officially a date, and they aren't defying their parents."

"Oh, that's sneaky," Dieter said.

"I want to see that play," said Liesel, with a hard look at Dieter.

"Not the opening, we won't," Dieter said. "I just get my guard salary. We can go see a matinee maybe, or watch the broadcast version." Often plays at the Grantville High theater were videotaped for later broadcast on the cable network that was also run from the high school.

May 7, 1632
Badenburg Tailor Shop

Bruno Schroeder ran the cloth tape measure up David Bartley's trouser leg while Johan stood three feet away, having one of Bruno's journeymen measure him. The cloth tape was an up-time device and highly prized, so Johan was being measured with a knotted string. Johan fought down his grin, then remembering his new dentures, let it show.

There was a drawing of a man in very full hose, a tight bodice and leather shoes with a brass or gold buckle. The hose were padded at the top to accent the buttocks, and David had been muttering about them, calling them diapers since he arrived. Johan knew that they were a style that was already out of fashion, replaced with the tighter and longer knee pants that were called breeches, but Karl Schmidt was going along with this style to appease his friend, Bruno.

Johan was feeling especially lucky, because even though he was staying on the board of the Higgins Sewing Machine Corporation, he was thought of as David's man, so he would not have to buy the very fancy outfit that David was getting. Johan would get a pair of up-time pants in dark green and a gray-brown jacket over a white blouse. He was also getting a cut that would let him get **to** his pistol easily, without making it obvious.

Bruno was going on about the importance of Karl Schmidt's and Ramona Higgins' wedding and how "You have to make a good impression for your mother's sake. It's not just going to be up-timers there, you know. Prominent down-timers from as far away as Eisenach will be there."

Johan was profoundly grateful that he didn't need to make a good impression.

June 2, 1632
Badenburg

Johan lifted the mug to his mouth and drank down a large swallow of the dark brown beer. He was a little drunk, but only a little, and besides, he wasn't nearly as angry at the world as he was back when he was a mercenary soldier.

"Director Kipper?"

Johan looked up. It was the mayor of Badenburg.

"Just the man I wanted to see." He came over to the table where Johan was sitting. It was an outdoor table, and it was loaded. There was a pig with an apple in its mouth, and in front of Johan was a large plate full of ham, coleslaw, and pickled beets. Next to the plate was a large chunk of bread with plenty of soft butter ready to hand.

The mayor sat on the bench beside Johan and then looked around severely. The pretty girl and the young man across from them got up and left. Johan would have preferred the young couple stay. The scenery was better, for one thing. Then the mayor breathed on him, a mixture of alcohol, garlic, and a lot of onion. Johan started looking for a way out.

"So, tell me about the mutual fund or investment bank that your young David is setting up."

Johan didn't have the least idea what the mayor was talking about, but he had played cards and dice for years and knew how to keep his countenance bland. He considered. It was clear that the mayor—who was no great friend of Karl Schmidt—thought something was up. The mayor was also normally no great friend of Johan. So Johan smiled a big, happy, smile and just as unconvincingly as he could manage, he said, "I have no idea what you're talking about, Mr. Mayor. I don't even know what a mutual bank or investment fund is."

The mayor's face clouded up. Johan knew that the mayor knew him well enough to know that after hearing the mayor say mutual fund and investment bank, Johan would not confuse the words. The mayor would be sure he was lying through his false teeth. But he wasn't. Johan had no idea what was going on.

"Director Kipper, I am the mayor of Badenburg and a major property owner. I have a right to know."

Johan shrugged is ignorance, and the mayor got up and left, displeased. Johan started to go back to his beer and his meal, but found that his appetite was on leave. He looked regretfully at the meal before him and went looking for David.

David was not to be found.

Hans, who was also at the wedding, said he had gone off with Karl Schmidt. "If I was just married, I wouldn't be talking to my stepson. I'd have better things to do."

"Me too," Johan agreed. Mistress Ramona was a very attractive woman. "But that's probably how rich people get rich."

Hans looked at Johan and Johan blushed. Between his salary as a director and his stock, Johan was a wealthy man. He just didn't think of himself that way. He was just old Johan, Master David's man. Which reminded him . . . he needed to find David.

For the next two hours, Johan Kipper looked for David Bartley and fended off questions about the investment bank and mutual fund that he didn't know a thing about. He managed to sound like he knew all about it but was being discreet. Then, some twenty minutes after Karl Schmidt and Ramona Higgins left for their wedding trip, he was called to the Schmidt house, where he met up with Frantz Kunze, David and the gang, and the mayor of Badenburg.

As Johan came into the room the mayor sniffed, and Herr Kunze said, "Don't be angry at Johan. He was just doing his job."

"I suppose he will be on the board of this new mutual fund, just like he is for HSMC," the mayor said grumpily.

"I suspect the Sewing Circle will insist on it," Kunze agreed.

And that was how Johan Kipper ended up on the boards of two of the largest corporations associated with the Ring of Fire, the Higgins Sewing Machine Corporation and Other People's Money.

Chapter 5—A Rising Tide Sinks Some Boats

July 22, 1633
Power Plant

"It's your damn fault," Darlene Myers screamed at Julie Marie Porter. "If I hadn't had to work, I'd have been home with Johnny and Jack!" She threw a half-full coffee cup at her boss' wife and the manager of the power plant, and then turned and ran out of the building.

"Damn," Julie said to Bill Porter, her husband. "I thought she was getting better." It had seemed that Darlene was adapting to the world as they'd all had to do. But Darlene was hardly the first up-timer who'd gone off the rails after the Ring of Fire. It took her a bit longer than most, but she probably wouldn't be the last, either.

"You know we have to fire her," Bill said.

"She probably won't come back," Julie said. "Partly because of embarrassment, but I think she really does blame me for making her work that day."

"Oh, come on, Julie. She asked for the overtime."

"I know, hon. But it's easier to blame me than to blame herself."

August 5, 1633
High School Cafeteria

Johan Kipper sat in the cafeteria in the high school, going over reports from OPM. He was on the board of the mutual fund and there was quite a lot of paperwork involved. He heard the rumble of teens in the distance and checked his watch. It was a down-time made pocket watch, made by a company that he was invested in. Sarah Wendell had put him into the stock, and the primary owner had given him the watch last Christmas.

Still, in many ways his job wasn't all that different from when he had first come to work for Mrs. Higgins. He was still haggler-in-chief for Master David's business projects. Johan grinned at the thought, showing a very nice smile. Dentures, of course, that had been paid for by Mrs. Higgins not long after he had gone to work for the family. He would have been able to pay for his own now, if you could still buy the up-time artificial resin-based dentures at all.

There was gray in his hair but there was still more brown than white, and he wasn't going bald. He was clean-shaven, clean in general, and well dressed. He was still no prize by up-timer standards but was a well enough formed man of the short and stocky sort. He still had the pock marks that were fairly common in the seventeenth century but that had virtually disappeared from the twentieth.

"Who are you and what are you doing here?" said a voice in up-timer English.

Johan looked up to see a short, brown-haired woman in a hairnet and apron, holding a great pot of knackwurst and sauerkraut, apparently today's lunch main course. All of which led him to believe that she was a down-timer lunchroom servant, but the language shouted up-timer. So did the clear, rosy complexion. Even after two years, the discontinuity made Johan a little uncomfortable, though he knew perfectly well that it shouldn't. She put the big tray in the steam table and gave Johan a look of increasing suspicion.

"I am doing paperwork," Johan said carefully.

"I could see that. Why are you doing it in the high school lunchroom?"

"I'm waiting for Master David," Johan said, fully aware that he was making a hash of the whole mess.

∞ ∞ ∞

Darlene Myers wished she had asked one of the other cafeteria workers about the man before she approached him, but he had just been sitting there, in a mix of up-timer and down-timer style clothing—rich clothing, good materials and tailored, if she was any judge. And she thought about all the stories from up-time about predators frequenting schools and assumed down-time had the same sort of creeps. And he looked sort of creepy, or at least he had at first glance. Now she was more than a little lost. Who was this Master David? Was there some down-time noble going to the high school? She realized that there must be. She hadn't thought about it, but she had just gotten this job a few days ago, through a friend who thought she was crazy to take it.

"Who is this Master David?" she asked. "Is he a student here?"

"Master David Bartley," the man said, with what sounded to Darlene like considerable pride in his voice. Now that sounded like an up-timer, not a down-timer. Though . . . No. She remembered the Higgins Sewing Machine Company and OPM. David Bartley was one of the up-timer kids who had started getting rich after the Ring of Fire. Apparently, David had gone native in a big way, servants and the whole deal. What Darlene wanted to do was send this servant off with a bee in his ear about the rights of man and give this David Bartley a good talking to on the same subject. The problem was, she didn't actually know anything about the situation.

So she gave the man a warning look and a *humpf* and retreated back to the kitchen to gather more intelligence.

∞ ∞ ∞

"Who is that guy in the serving room?" Darlene asked when she got back to the steamy kitchen. "He says he is waiting for *Master* David Bartley, no less."

Grete Hoffmann looked over at the calendar on the wall. "I bet it's the HSMC board meeting." Grete was a tall woman with blond hair fading to gray and a lined face that was splotchy in the heat of the kitchen. She wore a puffy white hat that fulfilled the function of a hairnet but was a bit cheaper and a white apron over a gray-brown blouse and skirt. Now she nodded in satisfaction. "Johan Kipper is on the board, you know. Even after the Schmidt takeover, he stayed on the board, along with Delia Higgins and Mr. Marcantonio."

Which didn't answer Darlene's question at all.

"What?"

Grete, an old Grantville hand and a great gossip, gave Darlene a condescending look. About half the kitchen staff here was convinced she was an idiot, otherwise what was she doing serving meals to teenagers when her up-timer knowledge was so valuable. Grete, after questioning her, just figured she was crazy.

"Well, it's like this. David Bartley is the real head of OPM and is one of the biggest stockholders in HSMC. Johan Kipper is his man. He represents David Bartley in board meetings and the like, because David Bartley is too young to sit on the board of a corporation by your up-timer law."

It really wasn't the sort of discussion that Darlene had expected from the kitchen staff of a high school lunchroom, but she hadn't thought about what the changes the down-time world had brought to Grantville would mean.

"How many of our students are millionaires?" Darlene wondered aloud.

"Oh, lots," Grete said and started going through the names.

"Never mind." Darlene interrupted the list. "Why does Herr Kipper—at least, I assume it's Herr Kipper out there—call David Bartley 'Master David'? Hasn't anyone mentioned to him that we don't have slavery in Grantville?"

For a minute Grete just looked at her like she was strange. "It's perfectly prop—" Grete stopped then continued, "He is just a little old-fashioned. Johan Kipper came to them as a former soldier, a beggar really, hoping for work, and now he is rich." Grete clucked her tongue at such undeserved good fortune. "Some people are just born lucky."

All this left Darlene confused, but very intrigued. She picked up another tray for the steam table and headed out to check out the guy. He wasn't a great looking specimen, short and stocky and with the leftovers from the worst case of acne she had ever imagined. No, she realized. Johan Kipper had survived smallpox. He was apparently as tough as he looked. "Is the board meeting of Higgins Sewing Machine Corporation coming up?" she asked, mostly because it was all she could think of to open the conversation with.

He looked up. "Yes. How did you . . ."

"Grete. She knows everything about everyone. At least she claims to. Why does that mean you need to be here?"

"Because young Master David needs to know what will be decided at the board meeting. Herr Schmidt is arguing again to increase the sales price."

"Why? Have costs gone up?"

"No. They have gone down. But we sell a sewing machine and, often as not, the buyer turns around and resells it the next day for a considerable profit."

"And Herr Schmidt figures you might as well make the extra profit."

"Yes."

"So, why not?" Darlene asked. "I mean, I can understand why you guys might want to be generous, but if the generosity isn't getting to the end-users, why not make the extra profit?"

Johan looked at her in confusion for a moment. "End-user? Oh, I get it! Very clever. Sometimes it takes me a minute to understand up-timer expressions. Young Master David is concerned that if we price the units too high we are likely to entice someone else to go into competition. Herr Schmidt insists that they will anyway, as soon as they can figure out how. He wants to guard our proprietary information more strongly." Johan grinned, an open, friendly expression, with just a touch of impishness. "A couple of weeks ago, he was threatening to lock the Partow twins out of the factory if they kept giving away secrets."

Darlene was finding this a very interesting conversation. She had been so busy the last couple of years, grieving for her husband and her son, Johnny, both left up-time, and trying to help reinvent electrical power generation over at the power plant, that she hadn't had much time to consider what was happening in the rest of Grantville. But she was more interested in what this man thought. "What do you think?"

"About the Partow twins?"

"No. About raising the price."

"I think Herr Schmidt is right about someone starting to build sewing machines as soon as they can, but I don't see any way of stopping them from learning how to do it. Too much is public record."

"So should you raise the price?"

Johan stopped and clearly gave Darlene's question some thought. "I think Herr Schmidt is right about the price."

"Are you going to tell David Bartley that?"

"Yes."

Then Grete came out of the kitchen and Darlene had to go back to work.

∞ ∞ ∞

Johan found himself somewhat distracted all during the lunch meeting with David and the rest of the Sewing Circle. They talked about the price hike and Johan did argue that they might as well increase the price. Sarah and David were opposed. In Sarah's case, Johan thought it was because she was starting to feel it was a bit immoral to overcharge like that. David, probably because he wanted to delay the competition as long as possible in order to get Higgins established as *the* name in sewing machines. The twins didn't care.

Finally, David gave in and Sarah, pouting, was outvoted.

Johan looked over at the door to the kitchen area and it wasn't Darlene Myers who came through it. When he looked back to the group around the table, David was looking at him and grinning. Johan felt his face heat and David's grin grew.

In spite of David's grin, the next time the door opened Johan looked again and this time it was Darlene. She came out and glanced over at the table they were at and Johan looked away to see David looking at Darlene. But at least David didn't bring up his observations in front of the rest of the group.

∞ ∞ ∞

Darlene went back out to the lunchroom to start clearing out the steam table. She was pretty engrossed on pulling the hot pans out without burning herself.

"Can I help you with that?" a voice asked and she jerked up.

"Oh! Ah, no. That's all right. It's my job, after all. How did your meeting go?"

"Well enough. The Sewing Circle will not oppose Herr Schmidt's price increase."

That was interesting. When this man decided something like that, he could persuade the kids.

"So, how often do you have these meetings?" Darlene asked. Maybe she'd cook something special for him and those kids.

"Every few weeks, or every month. It depends on how the businesses are going. HSMC, once a month, but OPM requires more meetings. And the others, well, it depends on if they need Master David's guidance."

"That means you'll be back, then?" Darlene hoped so. This was the first time in over two years that she'd seen someone who interested her as this man did.

"I'll be back, yes."

August 27, 1633
High School Cafeteria

"Who does Johan keep looking at in the lunch meetings?" Sarah Wendell asked a few weeks later. "And why is he coming to school so often?"

"Her name is Darlene Myers. I asked one of the cafeteria workers. Her husband and son, and her house, were left up-time. She worked in the power plant," David said.

"What is someone with that sort of knowledge doing on a serving line?" Sarah asked.

"She had a breakdown a while back. Which is why she's not working for the power plant, but as to why she's doing a joe job in the cafeteria, I

don't know, and it bothers me. Especially if Johan is interested in her."
David considered. "I think I should have her checked out. Which is
inconvenient as all-get-out, because guess who I would normally have
check her out."

"Johan. Ya, I get it, probably not a good idea this time," Sarah said.
"I'll ask around."

"Thanks. I'll have Leonhard look into it from the down-timer side."

"Do you realize how silly we sound? A couple of kids looking into
the background of someone Johan Kipper is interested in."

David nodded agreement, but he didn't actually agree. He wished
he'd been able to do it with some of the jerks his mom had dated up-time,
and Johan was rich now. Also, in David's opinion, Johan tended to look at
up-timers through rose-colored glasses.

August 30, 1633
Wendell House

Judy came into Sarah's room without knocking.

"Judy," Sarah complained, looking up from the work on her desk,
"can't you learn to knock?"

Judy rolled her eyes. "It's not like you're going to be doing anything.
Anyway, I got the scoop on Darlene Myers." She plopped onto Sarah's bed
and pulled out a notepad. Shorthand was back in vogue in the seventeenth
century. "Born 1967 so she's thirty-five. She was married, with one crumb
snatcher, both her hubby and the kid were left up-time. She worked at the
power plant and stayed on after the Ring of Fire. Everyone knew she was
having problems, but she seemed to be handling it. Trouble is, she didn't
talk to anyone about her problems; she just threw herself into her work."

Judy shrugged. She was familiar with the story; so was Sarah. It
wasn't uncommon in Grantville post Ring of Fire. "She trained three sets
of down-timers to do her job, then had a breakdown where she was

throwing things at her boss or the plant manager or someone. Quit or was fired. In any case, never went back.**"**

"The way I got it, indirectly from her brother Allen, she had a very hard time dealing with the loss of Jack and little Johnny, her up-time family, but she just wouldn't get help." Judy shook her head at such stupidity.

"Not everybody wants to talk about that kind of thing. It's a private sort of difficulty," Sarah pointed out. She sort of agreed with Judy's assessment, but thought that Darlene's self-treatment might be the right thing for her. Just be around people, not heavy equipment, for a while.

Judy rolled her eyes again.

"Leonhard told David that the down-timers she worked with found her pleasant, if a bit reserved. They were surprised when she 'quit' the power plant and went to work at the elementary school. They were more surprised when she said that working with all the younger children was too much. It reminded her of her lost son. So she transferred to the high school."

"So she was hit pretty hard by the Ring of Fire. Judy stood up and headed for the bedroom door. It wasn't an uncommon story. The Ring of Fire had hit a lot of people hard, and sometimes the ones that it hit hardest were the least willing to talk about it.

September 1, 1633
High School Cafeteria

"So where did you grow up?" Darlene asked, the next time Johan showed up for one of the pre-board meetings he had with the Sewing Circle kids. She wondered if Johan would notice her new hairdo and the bit of makeup she was wearing.

"Outside Amsterdam in the Low Countries. I was given some education, but not too much. My papa didn't want me getting above myself."

Apparently, he did notice. At least he was looking. "Why not?" Darlene asked. "I mean, wouldn't your father want you to rise as high as you could?"

Johan's expression changed. Darlene could tell he was trying to figure out how to explain. "Yes, but to Papa's way of thinking, as high as a person born into our family could properly go was chief servant, majordomo to a noble or merchant house. We weren't suited for anything else."

"That's horrible."

"That's what I thought. Which is why I ran away to the army at fifteen." His expression got sad. "Partly, anyway."

"Well, you've done a lot better than that. I bet he'd be proud of you."

"I'm not sure about that." Johan grinned. "He'd probably say I was reaching too far, really."

Darlene wondered if the man would ever reach for her, then was startled that she'd thought that. But she still wondered.

"Ah . . ." He stopped.

"Yes?" Darlene asked.

"I, ah, wondered if, perhaps . . . you might let me take you to the play at the high school next week. And maybe . . . dinner tonight?"

"Why, yes, Johan. I'd like that."

September 1, 1633
Marcantonio's Pizza Parlor

Johan held a chair for Darlene. Then, when she was seated, he went around the table and took a seat. Darlene noticed it was facing the main door and gave a view of the hall to the bathroom and to the counter where they fixed the pizza. Suddenly Darlene realized that every time she had seen Johan in the cafeteria, he was sitting somewhere where he could see the entrances and had his back facing toward a wall. He didn't make a big deal of it. It didn't even seem fully conscious on his part. She wondered what his life had been like.

The waiter came over and they ordered a pitcher of beer. Johan wanted a cheeseburger pizza, and Darlene agreed.

"I thought you might want a veggie pizza?" Darlene asked.

"No. I'm an old Grantville hand, and the meat rich diet that up-timers like is easy to get used to. Not that I ever had that much meat before I came to Grantville."

"Really? What did they feed you at that estate near Amsterdam?"

"Well, the kitchen servants and the personal servants got meat sometimes. But I was a third assistant footman. I got bread and cabbage soup with more soup than cabbage. Sometimes some cheese, if we were lucky."

"Jack hated cabbage and wouldn't touch sauerkraut. It was beef all the time, too. He didn't like chicken or pork much. I had a heck of a time figuring out what to feed that man. He'd have eaten steak every day if we could have afforded it. And Johnny was a lot like his dad—" Darlene stopped. She'd never intended to talk about Jack or Johnny with Johan, but here she was, doing just that.

Johan smiled, but there was a bit of a twist to it that was accented by the pockmarks on his right cheek.

"What?" Darlene asked.

"Nothing."

"No, really, Johan. It's something. I could tell from your face."

"It's just 'we couldn't afford steak every day.' But you had beef at every meal, or most of them. And you had *meals* every day. You up-timers were rich before the Ring of Fire even though you thought you were poor. No, don't misunderstand," Johan added quickly at what he saw on Darlene's face. "That's why I didn't want to say anything. I don't resent it. I'm not jealous. It's just a fact that up-timers know more and can do more, so you're richer. The amazing thing is that you seem willing to let us be richer too. It's just a little weird when we hear you talking about how poor you were up-time, even when you don't say it directly."

Darlene considered what he was saying and she guessed it was true. Then he asked. "What does your husband do?"

"You mean what did he do," Darlene said.

"You think he has changed so much?"

"I think—" Darlene stopped. "I think he's gone. I think the mass and energy that made him up is in a different form now, because of the Ring of Fire. The universe is a closed system and the—" Darlene stopped and searched for a word. "—stuff that made up my world has been reorganized to make a different world. The stuff to make our future has to come from somewhere."

"How do you know it's a closed system?" Johan asked.

"That's sort of what universe means. Everything, all there is, infinity. There can't be any more."

"I don't think so," Johan said. "I think that either you're using the wrong word to describe what happened and what it happened to, or you're not defining it right."

"What do you know about it?"

"Darlene, I've been living in Grantville since June of 1631. People have been discussing the Ring of Fire and what it means from one end of Europe to the other, and most of those discussions have been right here. Or at least been repeated here. Every servant with a mop bucket in Grantville knows all the theories. At least a lot of them. I've talked to the high school physics teacher and down-time philosophers about it. Read the stories in the newspapers and even read some of the learned treatises on it."

Darlene managed not to let her mouth hang open, but it was a near thing. It never occurred to her that— she wasn't sure what had never occurred to her. That down-timers would care, that people would have time to consider any of it. That someone like Johan could understand such things. She had been so sure that it had to be the way her nightmares portrayed it that she hadn't ever questioned it.

"What do you think happened?" she finally got out.

"I don't know," Johan admitted. "I *believe* that God did something special, and I choose to believe that he didn't murder a universe to do it. I have no proof of that, but I have no proof of the other, either. The idea that the universe is all there is, that's just an idea, it's not proof. I have no proof either way, so I'll go with what I feel."

Somehow, what Johan said made Darlene feel better. After that they talked more about their lives before the Ring of Fire. And Darlene realized over the course of the dinner that how bad she felt after the Ring of Fire was a reflection of how happy her life was back then. She had loved and been loved, and that was worth it all.

October 23, 1633
High School Cafeteria

Somehow, they had become each other's friendly ear. Darlene smiled as Johan came into the cafeteria, at least until she saw his expression. "What's wrong?"

Johan hesitated just a moment, then waved her over to a corner. "I have to go to Amsterdam."

"Amsterdam? Amsterdam is under siege, and the Netherlands are a war zone. Why would you need to go to Amsterdam?"

"Because Master David is going."

Now Darlene remembered, hearing about the guilder scare. Last month, right after the word of the siege had hit Grantville, David Bartley and Prince Karl von Liechtenstein had stepped in and bought up guilders.

To hear Grete tell it, all the guilders in Grantville. "Why did that idiot David have to go and buy a bunch of guilders, anyway?"

"Master David had his reasons," Johan insisted.

"What reasons?"

Johan was silent for a few beats then said, "It doesn't matter. What matters is that Master David is going to Amsterdam, and I have to go with him."

Darlene found Johan's devotion to the kid endearing, irritating, infuriating, insane, and a little creepy—all at once. She knew why Johan felt that way. He had told her about how David treated him and how Delia Higgins had given him a share in the sewing machine company and how David included him in OPM and the other deals he made. She knew that they had made him rich, but the way he doted on David was just wrong. And now the idiot boy was dragging him off to Amsterdam in the middle of a war. Johan had seen enough war to last a dozen lifetimes. And he didn't need to see any more, in Darlene's opinion. Not that she had any call to complain. They'd been dating less than a month.

Chapter 6 — Letters from Amsterdam

November 8, 1633
High School Cafeteria

"I have a letter for you, Ms. Myers," Trent Partow said.

"For me?"

"Yep. It's from Johan. It came in the pouch." He held out a sheet of folded paper. It had a string around it that was held in place with a wax seal.

"What pouch?" Darlene asked as she took the letter. The seal had an eagle on it. Darlene pointed at it. "What's this?"

Brent looked then shrugged. "Liechtenstein seal. Prince Karl probably let Johan use it. Anyway, the pouch is because the mission to Amsterdam is quasi-official. It doesn't exactly have diplomatic status, but they got the Cardinal-Infante's permission and the permission of the government before they left, so they have their own sealed pouches for private correspondence back here to Grantville."

"You mean Johan is like some sort of diplomat?"

"Sort of." Trent shrugged. "Brent and I are inventors. David's a mogul. Sarah's an economist. It's the Ring of Fire."

"And I am serving in a high school lunchroom."

"I know, ma'am, and, honestly, that seems a little weird. Especially considering how much you know about electronics."

Darlene had no idea what to say to that. But, thankfully, Trent didn't push it. He just gave her the letter and a wave, then went on his way.

It was later that afternoon when she finally got a chance to sit down, break the seal, and read the letter. Johan Kipper's handwriting was better than she expected, but the down-time education system, without even typewriters, was very much about good penmanship.

Dearest Darlene,

I may be overstepping my place with that greeting and if it gives offense I apologize most profoundly. But I miss you even more than I thought I would and the shield of paper the letter provides gives me courage to say what I have wanted to say since I met you. So:

My dearest Darlene,

We arrived in Amsterdam yesterday and have yet to meet the Cardinal-Infante. But I did get to see the estate where I was born, since it is outside the city proper. It has brought back memories. Some good, but more bad. We were not well treated, though not so harshly as in some places. But I remember my sister who was, she insisted, in love with the burgher's son. Never mind. The pain of those days is old, and both my sister and her child are dust. And the burgher's son, as well. Which is a good thing, else I would be tempted to foolishness.

I always resented the way they treated us, but assumed that was because they weren't real nobles, just burghers with a lot of money. Then I met real nobles in the army, and they were no better. It wasn't till the Ring of Fire that I found people who seemed to me worthy of loyalty. I know that you find the way I feel about young Master David and the rest confusing, but coming back here has brought it into focus. David is what the burgher and his family should have been but weren't. We are here not just to make money, but to save the guilder and so save the Netherlands and perhaps the rest of Europe. It's worth doing and I am pleased to be a part of it. I also will be glad to get back to Grantville. I find that I miss our conversations. I miss your insightful questions and your friendly smile. I know the loss of your family cut you deep and being here again reminds me of how deep and slow to heal such a loss can be. I understand your need to be around people but find myself wishing that you could find a position that let you be around people but still let you use more of your skills.

The letter went on to talk about how he felt about her and the world.

November 10, 1633
High School Cafeteria

A couple of days later, Darlene walked up to Trent Partow, who was chatting with a very pretty girl. As Darlene came near, the girl got up and, with a wave, left. As she left, Darlene realized she was Els Engel, Maid Marian from the radio show *Robin of the CoC*. By now Darlene was almost used to the students of Grantville High being big stars and captains of industry. Trent was dressed in a JROTC Major's uniform and looking quite spiffy. He also had a dreamy, distracted expression as he watched Els Engel leave.

Darlene coughed and Trent gave a start, then smiled at her. "Hey, Ms. Myers."

She gave Trent a letter, saying, "To go into the pouch for Johan." Trent took it and Darlene asked, "Has Johan mentioned my working in the cafeteria?"

"No. Why?" Trent asked.

"Because he said pretty much the same thing you did in his letter."

"About what?"

"About why am I working in the cafeteria when I ought to be working in electronics."

Trent shrugged a very teenage shrug, and said, "It's a pretty obvious question."

"It is if you know I worked in the power plant, but why would you know that if Johan wasn't talking to you?"

"Oh." Trent looked rather embarrassed. "David had you checked out. Because, well, Johan is rich now and that means a lot down-time."

It meant a lot up-time too, Darlene knew. Not to everyone, but to a lot of people. She'd read enough magazines before the Ring of Fire to know that pre-nups were pretty standard among the rich and famous. Still, the whole notion that she might be a gold digger was more than a little offensive. Especially because, well, she had noticed that Johan was rich, and it had had an effect. Along with the realization that he thought of her as someone who he could discuss matters of importance with, it made him seem more attractive and less threatening. She didn't figure he would have her out at the stream pounding his dirty clothes on rocks.

"I'm not sure how I would react if Johan had checked me out. But David Bartley? What the fuck business was it of his?" Darlene didn't usually curse, and especially not in front of kids, even teenagers. But suddenly she was really pissed off.

It was clear that Trent Partow didn't have a good answer to that, from his embarrassed look more than his silence. She humphed and gave him the letter anyway.

Trent thanked her and left, but that wasn't the end of it. An hour later, Brent Partow showed up. Brent looked like Trent but moved differently. He was more open and casual, less studied. He was even wearing jeans that were very faded and a little ragged at the cuffs. "David did it because he's Johan's friend and he cares. It wasn't an insult to you, because before he checked you out we didn't know who you were. Even if you had been a gold digger—and every single one of us has had experience with gold diggers since HSMC went public back in '31 and especially since

OPM—David wouldn't have tried to buy you off or treat you like Sabrina in the movie. He would have let Johan know and decide for himself." He grinned engagingly. "I should know. That's what he's done when one of my friends turns out to be after my money. Which happens more than you might think, Ms. Myers."

"Well, it's still insulting. And it's still none of his business," Darlene said, in spite of the fact that she saw Brent's point. "And if he wanted to know something, he should have had the guts to ask me to my face."

"Maybe. All right. In that case, I have a question to ask you to your face. What are you doing slopping the high schoolers when you could be teaching down-timers how to build electrical components and gauges? Do you have any idea how important electricity is to this world?"

"Well . . . you know . . . the thing is . . ." Darlene stopped.

Brent just waited.

"Well . . ." Darlene hadn't thought about it from the point of view of the rest of the world. "I just . . . I was so tired. And sick. Just sick of everything. All I could think about was Jack and Johnny. . . . and I didn't crack up till I had trained replacements."

Brent nodded. Darlene guessed that was in the briefing they'd gotten. "I'm sorry about your family," he said. "I was lucky. I had a lot of friends who were left up-time, but most of my family was here. I know it was worse for people who lost family. I think you ought to talk to someone about it. It's not just the opportunities for yourself that are getting lost. It's what you can do for the world. Look, Ms. Myers, I know a bunch of people think of David as some sort of Scrooge or maybe J.P. Morgan or something, but the truth is that he, all of us, do this stuff because it's important. Not because it makes us rich. That's just a byproduct."

"Not a bad byproduct," Darlene said.

"I'm not complaining, true. Back up-time, I'd never have been this kind of rich. But, more importantly, I'd never have been able to build the things I've built. The washing machine has made life easier for hundreds of people—heck, probably thousands of people. The generator packages we're working on—and that's something you could help with—why, those are going to improve even more lives. And improve them more."

Darlene was intrigued in spite of herself. "What sort of generator packages?"

Brent snorted. "That's the trouble. You can't just build a generator, or a toaster, or a light bulb. The toaster and the light bulb need the generator and the generator isn't a lot of use without the toaster or the light bulb, or something to power. And then there's the question of getting the mechanical motion to run the generator."

Darlene started nodding, because this was basically what she'd been doing at the power plant, or at least part of it. "So how are you working it out?"

"Not as well as we'd like. It takes a lot of fiddling. We can't build a standard system, like the sewing machine or the washing machine. We have to fit each one to the use it's to be put to. And that makes it more expensive. We need to standardize as many of the components as we **can** so they can fit into a customized system. We've been doing that one component at a time, as we develop them. Then selling them off to other companies to mass produce."

"What sort of components?"

"Well, the toaster I mentioned and an electric space heater. Small electric motors to power things like down-time made food processors. But we also have to make fuses and switches so that the little electrical systems we put in houses and factories don't burn out because too much is plugged into them or too little. We are working on better lead acid batteries. Well, a village just outside the Ring of Fire is doing those, but we are having to buy them by the rack. Which makes the systems more expensive, but we have to have something to balance the output of the generators."

"Have you tried gyroscopes?" Darlene couldn't help asking. She knew that, up-time and down-time, the power plant had used great big gyroscopes to balance power requirements with generation and keep the system from blowing.

"Now see," Brent said with an impish grin, "that's why you're needed. Your understanding of this stuff. It's not stuff that down-timers can't learn, and I know you taught it to down-timers before you quit the power plant. But there are always more down-timers to learn it. And more ways to apply it. Have you considered a job at one of the research firms . . . like, say, Twinlo Park?"

"You're trying to recruit me?"

"Sure. Why not?"

"I thought you thought I was a gold digger."

"Nope. We wanted to find out if you were a gold digger. There is a difference. And while we were looking, we found out you have knowledge we need."

"Are you sure that this isn't a way to buy me off?"

"Absolutely not!" Brent said with such overdone offended dignity that Darlene knew he was joking.

Darlene didn't accept the job offer. Not then. She liked cooking and she had learned that she liked cooking for large numbers. She didn't want to go back to a job in a lab, spending her time assembling parts and soldering itty-bitty wires.

November 15, 1633
Amsterdam

Johan Kipper got Darlene's first letter with considerable pleasure. She hadn't objected to his heading. Instead, hers had echoed it: My dearest Johan!

Meanwhile there were products to buy, arrangements to be made. The craftsmen in Amsterdam were starved for work and the negotiations were going well. More importantly, Don Fernando's army was in real need of things like cheap sewing, clothes washing, and all sorts of other things that an army needed to keep in good repair. Johan Kipper, as David Bartley's man, had just the sort of stuff they needed and couldn't get, or at least was a lot more expensive when done by hand than when done by machine.

November 17, 1633
Amsterdam

The packet boat had arrived that morning, and the bag had a second letter from Darlene. However, it had taken a bit more time to follow them through the lines to Amsterdam proper. Johan was sitting in the house of David Heesters when the pouch caught up with them. He sat in the large stuffed chair and started to read.

Darlene wasn't pleased to learn that young Master David had checked her out. For that matter, Johan's first reaction wasn't one of unalloyed joy. But considering how many gold diggers he had discovered going after one of his charges—even little Master Donny, Master David's younger brother . . . His second reaction was to wonder what David had found. He finished the letter, then went to seek Master David, who was chatting with Herr David Heesters. "Might I have a word?" Johan asked.

Master David looked over at the older man. "I think we're done for now, Herr Heesters, aren't we?"

"If you like. I still want to talk more about getting the carding plant up and running, but that can wait."

Once they were on their own, Johan asked, "What did you find out about Darlene, Master David? Oh, and by the way, she is not happy with you."

"I'll write her with an apology," David said, then shrugged. "I didn't find anything all that dire anyway. She's not a spy for Richelieu or a denizen of Club 250. She seems to be one of the people who had real problems because of the Ring of Fire. Her husband and son were left up-time and she didn't get help with that grief. She just buckled down and did her job. By a few months ago, she was a burnout case at the power plant and quit to go to work in the school cafeteria, but the little kids at the elementary school were too much like her little boy. So she switched over to the high school. She had some pull to get the job, I think. There were dozens of down-timers who were actually better qualified to work in a large kitchen."

"Darlene said she likes to cook," Johan pointed out.

"Sure, and apparently she does a decent job. But someone, who was the chief cook for a down-time school or mine or whatever, where they had to feed lots of people, had more of the sort of experience needed for working on a school lunch line, even if they would need lessons on the up-time equipment. Besides, she does know about electrical instruments." David shook his head. "Never mind. It's not that big a deal. It just seems to me that she is wasting her talents and training."

Johan wasn't sure that he didn't agree with that, but it was Darlene's choice, not Master David's.

November 20, 1633
Amsterdam

Johan turned to fit through the narrow door into the attic apartment. It was on the third floor, just below the roof of the building, and it was packed with spinning wheels and women of all ages.

While David, Herr Wendell, Prince Liechtenstein and the rest were talking with the high and the mighty, Johan Kipper was in places like this, talking with the craftsmen and small business people of Amsterdam.

"What is this project you have in mind for my shop, Herr Kipper?" Herr Kikkert, a bouncy little man, hopped about the room like the frog he was named for, looking at the thread on the spinning wheels.

"Spinning thread," Johan answered.

"We already spin thread, Herr Kipper. Are you going to show us how to spin it into gold?" Kikkert asked, grinning, and one of the women giggled. "Normally, I would be thrilled with such an endeavor, but just at the moment I would rather see a way of spinning thread into ham hocks or sides of beef."

Johan laughed. "Granted, and I wish I could teach you that. No, actually I'm here for what I want you to figure out and teach us. We need more thread—wool, hemp, cotton, even silk. With the sewing machines, it takes much less time to make clothing, so more people are buying clothes and the price of fabric goes up. But the weavers can't make more fabric without more thread to weave. We have two shops working on the problem back in Grantville and one in Magdeburg, and those aren't the only ones. The first people to figure a way to spin more thread faster are going to get rich. So we have several projects, trading information back and forth. All with an agreement to share information with each other."

"What does this have to do with me and my ladies, my spinsters?" Herr Kikkert waved at the women who were at their wheels but were not doing much spinning at the moment. "We already make a lot of thread. Not that we have anyone with the money to buy it right now. The weavers have warehouses full of cloth and no money to buy thread to make more."

Johan knew that Kikkert was exaggerating. The siege hadn't been in place all that long. There hadn't been time for the weavers still in Amsterdam to fill up their warehouses or even run out of money. Though they would run out of money sooner than they would fill up the warehouses. But Johan had a cure for that. "You need something to work on, something that will provide employment for you and your spinsters. And who knows more about spinning than spinsters?"

Johan pulled up his briefcase, a down-time made one which Johan thought was better quality than the few real up-time ones that had come back in the Ring of Fire. It was also much less expensive than the real up-time made ones, but it very much looked like an up-time made briefcase, especially with the little combination lock built in. He moved the numbers to the appropriate postings and snapped the briefcase latch open. All theater, there wasn't really anything all that secret in the case. He pulled out a file. "Up-time they had great factories that made hundreds of miles of thread in a few hours, operated by only a few workers."

While Johan had been opening his case, the spinsters had gathered around. Now one spoke up. "That would put us out of work. Now I know why the Spaniard let you through. It was to destroy our spirits by killing our futures. I'm going to report you to the Committees of Correspondence."

Johan smiled at the woman with his even, white, false teeth and said, "Say hello to Gretchen for me, but don't worry about your jobs. There will be better ones coming. Working in a garment factory with a sewing machine is probably a step up from spinning. And there are other up-timer jobs, assembly line jobs. There is work in Thuringia now, more work than there are people to do it." Johan didn't think he was exaggerating too much, but he knew that if the spinning machines were produced, some of these women would be left out in the cold by the new machines. But Johan had, in forty years as a soldier, killed people for causes much less worthwhile.

They gathered around and went over the drawings and the tricks that had been discovered. Great improvements in carding had already been managed, but spinning was still running into problems. Johan wished Brent or Trent was here to explain the problems or, better yet, Rob Jones, an Englishman who had gone to work for them on the spinning project.

∞ ∞ ∞

"How was your day?" David asked him, tiredly, that evening.

"It went fairly well. The spinning shop will take on the project and several of the women there seemed to have some interesting ideas. It will be worth a try, and even if we get it first in Grantville or Magdeburg, it will still give us a place in Amsterdam to put the new spinning machines when they are worked out."

David nodded. "We'll need that, whoever gets a working model."

"Besides, it will give them employment," Johan added. "That has to be the hardest part of a siege for the townsfolk. Well, aside from the starving and the dying in the end, that is."

David snorted.

∞ ∞ ∞

Johan's next letter to Darlene was mostly about the excursions into Amsterdam. The spinning project was only one of the problems being worked on. And OPM had all those Dutch guilders to spend. He added:

> I understand your being upset about Master David's actions, but I must admit that if the situations were reversed I would have done the same thing. In fact, I have. In so doing, I have discovered both venality and nobility. People who saw David as a meal ticket, and people who had only the noblest of motives. The only way to learn was to look. So I hope you will forgive him and me for the actions that our situation demands.

Then he went back to telling her about the people of Amsterdam and the siege.

> I have seen sieges from both sides, as besieger and besieged, but in both cases I was in the army and had my duty. Mostly the civilians were just sort of there in the background. But this is different. I

think it's because of Gretchen Richter and her Committees of Correspondence. But the people are involved here. Morale is high on both sides. It is interesting to talk to a Spanish sergeant in the morning and a Dutch Committee guard guarding the walls in the afternoon. Boredom is a sap on morale, but the Committees have everyone working on maintenance or repairs. And the Spaniards are sure of their commander and eventual victory.

Johan went on to tell Darlene about several of the people he had met and about their lives and hopes.

November 25, 1633
Grantville, Myers Home

Darlene laid down the letter and considered. She was still working in the cafeteria, but starting to feel a bit guilty about it. There were people under siege in Amsterdam and the New U.S.—or, rather the State of Thuringia-Franconia as part of the USE—was caught in a war and she was, as Brent Partow insisted on calling it, slopping the teens.

But the truth was, she didn't like fiddling with little bits of wire, and she did like cooking. And, oddly enough, she found cooking for large numbers easier than cooking for one or a few. She wouldn't mind consulting a bit about electric parts now and then, but she didn't want to spend her time hand assembling poor copies of up-time gauges. Still . . . maybe she ought to start looking around for something she could do that used a little more of the knowledge she had as an up-timer.

A few hours later, a discussion with Trent Partow at the cafeteria added weight to something she got from Johan before he left, and even a little bit from the down-timers she had trained at the power plant.

"It's not the stuff that we know we know, mostly," Trent said. "It's the stuff we know that we don't even realize matters. Imagine having to build an airplane—or a crock pot, for that matter—just from books. Even good books. Not knowing why any of the parts were needed, not knowing what could be left out or what just looked unimportant." He shook his head. "I've tried to turn it around a couple of times. Imagine trying to shoe a horse from directions in a book. A book will tell you how many nails to use, but it probably won't tell you what is going to piss the brute off and have him kick you through the stall door. A lot of the time a down-timer, even—well, especially—a very smart down-timer, will come to me with something that doesn't work when she is sure it should work, and it's because she knows how water flows but not how water in a channel is different from electricity in a circuit. Or something like that."

They talked about the problems that Trent was having with mass producing electrical components. Basic stuff, like switches and dials. "So," Trent said, a few minutes later, "do you want a job?"

"What?"

"Do you want a job helping us develop cheap, efficient ways of mass producing electrical components?"

"No. I want a job cooking," Darlene said. "I wouldn't mind consulting on components now and then as needed, but I want to cook, not fiddle with tiny little parts."

Trent nodded. "I'll see what I can come up with."

Trent considered the middle-aged woman. Twinlo Park had its own power, produced by its own generators, and had natural gas from a well in Grantville in a tank on the premises, but people, if they ate at midday, either brought their lunch or went off to an inn in Badenburg, Bechstedt or one of the other little villages for lunch. It wasn't that far even to Badenburg, and they had some transport. But now that he thought about it, it might be a very good idea to have a cafeteria or restaurant or something out at the park. Besides, she knew her stuff, even if she wasn't all that good at doing wiring, according to her old boss at the power plant.

Which didn't matter, really. Twinlo Park had craftsmen who could make anything out of copper wire. Anything at all. An up-timer kitchen manager with knowledge of electronics to look at the stuff they made and give opinions . . . that might be really valuable. Besides, Johan Kipper was sort of part of the family.

"Like I said, let me look into it," he finally said to Ms. Myers.

November 26, 1633
Twinlo Park

"How about a restaurant?" Trent asked, as he walked into the front office of the main building at Twinlo Park. This wasn't the place where the stuff got made. This was the place that handled the paperwork.

Herr Josef Kunze looked up from the report he was reading. Josef was a cousin of Franz Kunze, the chairman of the board of OPM. He had been planted on them by Franz Kunze and their mother to make sure they didn't do anything dangerous.

Josef had horn-rimmed glasses. The rims were up-time made plastic and the lenses were down-time ground glass. They made his eyes look a bit smaller than they actually were. As nannies went, Josef was all right. He was smart enough to know what he didn't know and was willing to learn from kids. He kept the books for Twinlo Park and charged for their time when they got called in to consult. He paid the salaries of the staff and generally ran the place.

"What about a restaurant? Are you asking about a power plant for a restaurant?"

"No. I mean, what about putting a restaurant here at the park. We have the room since we haven't expanded into all of the buildings here."

Kunze was shaking his head. "There are only twenty employees. That's not enough people to make it profitable."

"No, I mean we could provide meals for the employees."

"Why should we? You know we have dozens of applicants. We don't need to offer perks like that."

Kunze, Trent noted, *was quite fond of up-time slang.* "I disagree. Part of this place, a big part of it, is the culture. We take care of our people here. That's policy, and you know it."

"And we do. We provide medical and injury insurance. We help our employees find lodging and more. Why have you suddenly decided that we need to feed them lunch too? It is only lunch you're talking about? Or are you planning on feeding them breakfast and dinner as well?"

"I hadn't thought about it, but yes, breakfast and dinner as well, if they want it. If they are here for breakfast before work, you know they are going to start talking about their projects while they eat."

Herr Kunze stopped to consider, and Trent waited for him to think it through.

"That would be a benefit. And if we were to provide a restaurant on the premises, breakfast and dinner might partially pay for themselves in extra work while they are eating. It's how this group works. But that doesn't explain why you have developed this sudden interest in having a restaurant in the park."

Trent grinned. "I need it to tempt in an expert on dials and switches. Johan Kipper's up-timer lady friend."

Johan Kipper was a name to conjure with, Trent knew. As David's man, he sat on the boards of OPM and HSMC plus at least a dozen other companies in which OPM had a major interest. He was very high up in the hierarchy of the Ring of Fire industrial community, at least the down-time side of it. Josef Kunze had gotten this job because he was Franz Kunze's cousin. He was competent and, in fact, good at it, but he never would have gotten it without connections. That was how the down-time world worked, and by now Trent was pretty sure that it was how the up-time world had worked too. Josef wasn't going to balk at giving a job to a *friend* of Johan Kipper.

"I would be happy to provide any friend of Herr Kipper with employment. However, inventing not just a job, but a whole new department—probably with at least a couple of employees—just to give her a job? Even if she is an up-timer?"

"Remember, she is an expert on dials and switches," Trent reminded him.

"So why not hire her as that?"

"Because she doesn't want that job," Trent said. "She likes to cook."

November 28, 1633
Twinlo Park

Josef checked out the woman on his own, then approved the plan. He had several reasons. One was the fact that Johan Kipper was not, in any sense, someone he wanted to get on the wrong side of. Kipper could end your career and, if necessary, your life. He was, to many down-timers, the iron fist in David Bartley's silk glove.

But another reason was that they really did need someone with an up-timer's understanding of electronics. Also, a little research had suggested that providing free meals to the employees would make them more productive.

Twinlo Park wasn't quite like an up-time research and development facility. As often as not, families were hired as a unit. Husband and wife, and occasionally children, came to the shop and worked together. Sometimes it was men and women who were not yet financially secure enough to marry after all the disruptions of the war. They had three couples, masters at their trades and their wives, who had lost their homes and hopes in the war, and now worked at Twinlo Park as a unit.

A restaurant on the premises would be of really great benefit, and not all that expensive.

Chapter 7 — Darlene's Restaurant

December 1, 1633
Twinlo Park

hat exactly do you want?" Darlene asked. "Do you want a down-time style tavern, a cafeteria or a real restaurant?"

"I'm not certain, Frau Myers. I have eaten in the Plaza Room in the Higgins and at Marcantonio's Pizza place, as well as some of the other restaurants of Grantville, but, honestly, I don't understand the difference between a tavern and a restaurant all that well," Josef Kunze said.

Darlene remembered eating at a Golden Corral in Morgantown before the Ring of Fire. It was sort of a cross between a cafeteria and a restaurant that called itself a buffet restaurant. And as Darlene thought about it, she figured that would probably be the way to go, especially if she could get a good handle on what the people at Twinlo Park liked. She could have most of the meals pre-made and ready and just put them out. Salads, soups, bread, and a couple of entrees; then, if someone wanted something special, they could order it. Yes, that would work. And while she was thinking all this, she realized that she had taken the job. At least in her own mind.

Darlene, like most up-timers, was not a good negotiator. She hadn't grown up in a world where all, or even most, prices were negotiable. It left her and most of the up-timers at a real disadvantage in dealing with down-timers who had probably negotiated the price of the first thing they had ever bought and most of the rest of their purchases. On the other hand, she was anything but stupid, and she could figure out why she was getting this job. It wasn't because she was an up-timer. It was because she was thought to be Johan Kipper's girlfriend. Darlene let a smile slip out. "I think that a buffet restaurant would be the best plan. I will leave my compensation to you and talk it over with Johan in my next letter."

Josef Kunze swallowed and Darlene felt her smile grow a little bit. Johan was such a nice man. She really didn't understand why he scared people like Josef Kunze so much.

December 7, 1633
Amsterdam

Johan Kipper laughed out loud when he read the part of Darlene's letter describing her negotiating with Herr Kunze, who Johan privately thought of as "the little Kunze," even though he was actually larger than Franz. He would show the letter to Franz at the next opportunity.

Young Master David, as it happened, was reading of the same general events, but in a letter from Trent Partow. "Trent writes that Darlene can make a mean fried rice and she went with this sort of German oriental style. But the food is from all over. There are baked potatoes and . . ." The list of foods was surprisingly varied, and apparently Darlene had hired two support chefs, a baker and someone named Grete who made the most delicious soups. And best of all, Trent's letter burbled, someone had finally found pepperoni that almost tasted like real pepperoni, and the color was almost right, so the pepperoni rolls they were making were almost as good as the ones back up-time.

"Your Darlene seems to be fitting right in, Johan," David said with a grin. By now the splitting of the Wisselbank was agreed on and the party was getting ready to head to Antwerp to see to the installation of the radios that would connect the two branches of the bank. Trent can't stop talking about the food and patting himself on the back for hiring her."

"I imagine Josef Kunze is still complaining about the expense." Johan smiled back. "Apparently, Darlene threatened him with me."

There was a snort from across the room. "You have taken horrible advantage of my cousin," Franz Kunze said. "But the cost will be coming out of the profits of Twinlo. How much of Twinlo do you own, Johan?"

Johan considered. He had helped the twins set up the park, along with Franz and OPM. OPM owned forty percent, the twins owned forty percent, Johan had gotten three percent for his help, and the rest was spread out among the twin's family. "Not that much, Franz, but I wouldn't be worried about the cost of the . . ." Johan looked back at the letter. " . . . buffet restaurant. It will pay for itself, I think. Especially since Darlene is complaining about not having time to cook because of all the electrical doodads that they make her look at."

"Is it a serious problem?" David asked.

"No, I don't think so. It's hard to tell just from the letter, but I think she actually enjoys it as long as she doesn't have to do the wiring."

"Back to our real business: what about the guilders?" Franz interrupted, bringing the conversation to their purpose. "What are we investing in besides the spinning problem?"

"Well, your interference in the siege hasn't helped," Johan complained. "Now that the craftsmen have access to a market for their goods, they are less interested in whiling away their time on learning to make up-timer products. Not *un*interested, but not nearly so desperate for work as they were when we got here."

"Fine. We're ruining your scam," David said, not sounding particularly sorry. "But what have you invested us in?"

"Shipping," Johan said.

"What?"

"I brought designs for fiberglass production and showed them pictures of fiberglass hulls, down at the shipyards.

"They can't sail their ships out, so there is no market for them just now. Even Don Fernando isn't letting them sail ships in and out of Amsterdam at the moment." Johan, while mostly pleased by the situation they had been able to support here in Amsterdam, found his sense of propriety somewhat outraged by a siege in which the besiegers were buying their boots and uniform tunics from the besieged. It was just not the way a siege should be carried out.

December 15, 1633
Twinlo Park

"They are in Antwerp," Sarah Wendell complained to Darlene over a bowl of mutton fried orzo. Which Darlene seasoned as much like beef fried rice as she could, except she added a bit of mint and some honey for sweetness. Mutton fried orzo had turned out to be one of her most popular dishes with the crew at Twinlo Park and increasingly with people who found a reason to drop in for the food. The Twinlo Palace provided free buffets for breakfast, lunch and dinner for employees of Twinlo Park, but anyone could come in, pay ten American dollars, and have all they could eat. By now they were serving thirty people at most meals. It was a very fortunate thing that Josef had insisted on a large dining room, even if he had done it so that there would be room for more employees as the research and development center grew.

"I know. I got another letter from Johan. Why them?" Darlene said. She and Sarah had found themselves in a similar circumstance, since Sarah was dating David and Darlene was sort of dating Johan. Sarah was more than a little resentful of David's getting to go when she didn't, and Darlene figured there was trouble on the horizon for the kids, but it wasn't her business. Darlene didn't resent not getting to go to Amsterdam, but she did worry about Johan a lot more than she had expected to when he left.

"I don't know. David insists they are the only ones that the Cardinal-Infante and the duke of Orange could agree on, but I think they just figured to get all the use out of the up-timers they could manage. The radio towers are expensive, even if they are using an existing building for a lot of the height."

"Sure. But Johan isn't going to be building any radio towers."

"Neither is David," Sarah agreed, then visibly considered. "It's probably HSMC and OPM. I bet the cardinal is looking to get up-time tech for the Spanish Netherlands. He knows that David and Herr Kunze are running OPM. If OPM decides to put, say, a light bulb factory in Antwerp, it won't hurt the cardinal's tax base any."

"It's weird to think of Johan that way," Darlene admitted. "Whenever he talks about himself, it's always not about himself. If you know what I mean."

"I haven't got a clue."

"It's 'young Master David put me on the board of OPM to represent him and the other members of the Sewing Circle.' Or 'and Mrs. Higgins put me in charge of the guard force for the Higgins Hotel.' It's never 'I am on the board of OPM' or 'I am in charge of the guards at the Higgins Hotel and at the Higgins warehouse.' It's even 'young Master Donny listens to me on matters of down-time custom.' Never 'I explained to little Donny that he's not supposed to kiss the girls and make them cry.' "

Now Sarah nodded. "I know. There is a whole range of responses we get, even from the down-timers who like us. We have Gretchen Richter, who has become more up-timer than up-timers on the subject of equal rights for all. Then you have Johan, who can barely manage to give lip service to the notion. He thinks of up-timers as nobles, the real nobles, the ones who behave the way nobles are supposed to. The ones, not to put too fine a point on it, that God put here. At first David tried to argue him out of it. Then he just sort of gave up. Besides, Johan is a heck of a lot more of a father to David than his dad ever was. He figures if that's the way Johan wants to be, then that's the way he can be."

"Pretty convenient for David to have Johan trotting around after him," Darlene said, feeling resentful of Johan's absence and blaming David for it.

"Look, Darlene, I know you're older and wiser than a teenage girl . . . but the down-timers have different rules. And Johan Kipper has been learning those rules for fifty years and more. Expecting him to throw them all away in a few days or even a few years . . . well, it ain't going to happen. It's not that David asked Johan to act the way he does. It's Johan. And David respects him enough to let him, even when it makes David uncomfortable. And it does. If you want any kind of relationship with Johan, David is part of the package, because Johan has picked David as his lord and that's all there is to it."

December 29, 1633
Antwerp Docks

The fog was thick enough to walk on, and it had been for a good part of their time in Antwerp, but the mission to Amsterdam boarded the packet boat that would take them to Hamburg in generally good spirits.

"I'll be glad to get back home," David Bartley said. "I'm getting way behind in my school work."

"We knew that was going to happen from the start, Master David. Though I admit we've spent more time on this than we expected," Johan said. "It was worth it, though, so far as OPM is concerned. We managed to make a good start on several businesses, and with the goods we've bought here and in Amsterdam we have more than doubled our initial investment in guilders." Johan was grinning happily. That they had bought those guilders with a low interest loan from the Fed didn't bother him at all, and he suspected it didn't bother young Master David either. There would be significant bonuses for both of them when the annual report came out.

That was important to Johan because, well, if a man was thinking about getting married it helped if he had the wherewithal to support a family. He would have something to show Darlene, something to prove she was getting more than a serving man. Even if he was young Master David's serving man and happy to be so.

December 31, 1633
Packet Boat

Fletcher Wendell grinned at Johan. "Well, up-time women are just as practical as down-time women, but they like to pretend they are romantics. So you want to go with the whole romantic part first, you know." Then, seeing Johan's face, he added, "Well, maybe you don't know. You take her out to a romantic dinner, kneel on one knee, present her with an engagement ring, and ask her to honor you by accepting your proposal of marriage."

By this time Johan was looking a little green, and Fletcher was having a grand old time. He kept elaborating on the proposal and adding bells and whistles till Johan caught on that he was being teased.

Then Fletcher backtracked a bit. "Remember, I said they like to pretend that they are ruled by romance, not that they truly are. I guess the biggest difference is that it's easier for a woman to say no if she wants to because she is less dependent on the prospects of the guy than down-time women are. For that matter, the guys are less likely to end up asking the girl on the basis of her prospects. I think it's just because we were richer up-time. We could afford to follow our hearts, not that our hearts were always right either.

"Look, just ask her and let her know it's truly what you want, not just what's practical."

January 4, 1634
Grantville Train Station

Darlene was there to meet Johan when the train pulled in. The weary travelers debarked, and David waved Johan toward Darlene and went to meet the rest of the group that had gathered to welcome them home. And there was Johan, coming toward her and slowing as he came. Darlene started to get nervous because she wasn't sure if he was slowing because he was just as nervous or because he had maybe changed his mind about her.

Darlene got more and more nervous as Johan slowed, till she couldn't take it anymore. And then she was moving. Three quick steps and he was within reach. Johan was a short man, though he didn't look it, and Darlene was actually a couple of inches taller than he was. And she was wearing two inch heels. She reached around, grabbed him in a hug and bent down to kiss him, not at all sure that he would respond, but unwilling to wait to find out.

He responded. His arms went around her and he returned her kiss with great fervor and moderate skill.

"I've missed you!" Darlene murmured into his mouth.

They were interrupted by applause and catcalls from the other people on the platform, and Darlene noted that Johan had a rather blotchy blush that went all the way up to his hairline and down somewhere past his collar. It wasn't, objectively, the most attractive blush she had ever seen, but she found herself wondering how far down it went.

January 10, 1634
Twinlo Park

"So where do you want to get married?" Darlene asked as she snuggled up to Johan.

"What do you mean? In Grantville, I guess."

"No, I mean, in what church? Or do you want a civil ceremony?"

Johan had been a Calvinist before he joined the army, and since then had been whatever faith was expected in the service he was a part of. In truth, he had lost his faith during his first real battle and never found it again. Until he came upon the Ring of Fire and the people it had brought into the world. That had convinced him—again—that God did exist and did care about the welfare of the world. What it hadn't convinced him of was any doctrine. Predetermination seemed to Johan at this point to be a totally discredited doctrine. "I don't know," he said. "What about you?"

"Well, my family was Presbyterian before the Ring of Fire but we weren't much on going to church. After the Ring of Fire, I was much too busy hating God for what he had done to my life to look very seriously at what the Ring of Fire meant in regard to the doctrines of my faith." Darlene stopped, and Johan waited while she worked it out. "I think the whole Calvinist predestination thing is right out the window. God can change our destinies any time he wants and He . . . or She . . ." she added, watching Johan's face carefully.

It wasn't the first time Johan had heard the idea of God perhaps being female. A few of the up-time women were adamant about it. Mostly, Johan thought, to piss off down-time men. So he said, "Or She," quite agreeably, and Darlene humphed.

"And if She can do it here on Earth, She can do it in heaven as well."

Johan nodded his agreement. "It would have been nice of Him . . . or Her, to give us some indication of what was expected of us, though."

"Yes, it would. But maybe He did," Darlene said. "He could have picked the Vatican, after all. Dropped the up-time Vatican or Brigham Young University, or some Buddhist temple here in this time. Instead, we get a mostly, but not entirely, Christian town with us all living together."

"So perhaps the message is stop killing each other over the small stuff," Johan said, nodding agreement.

"Maybe. And maybe we should look for a church that thinks that way to get married in."

"I think I know one. The Schmidt family, including young Master Donny, go to a church in Badenburg which is nominally Lutheran, but Pastor Steffan Schultheiss has converted it to what Mrs. Higgins calls passionate unitarianism. God will find a way into your heart no matter what faith you hold, so look for the commonalities and be kind to one another as you would hope for God to be kind to you. Mistress Ramona says it's very spiritual."

"Well, we could talk to him, anyway," Darlene said.

February 15, 1634
Badenburg

Pastor Steffan waved Darlene and Johan to chairs in the home he shared with his family. He looked a little harried, but said, "I'm glad that you two have found each other."

"So are we," Darlene said, smiling.

Johan watched with more cynicism than was really warranted. He knew about the pastor's revelation, and that it hadn't been universally accepted. Pastor Steffan's Revelation, as several people were calling it— complete with the capitalization—had offended a bit less than half the congregation, so he had kept his position. Barely. But it had also attracted followers, and while some had left, more had joined.

It was nice that he had made time to see them. At the same time, Johan knew that it was something of a coup for the pastor. He had performed the marriage of Karl Schmidt and Ramona Higgins. Now he was going to perform the marriage of Johan and Darlene. It gave him a certain status in Badenburg and meant that people would be slower to criticize his doctrine.

His wife came in with a tray of small sandwiches and a pot of tea. Then they got down to a discussion of the details. Everyone in the room had scheduling conflicts. Both Johan and Darlene had jobs and Pastor Schultheiss had a full calendar of weddings and christenings.

It took three little cheese sandwiches and a half a cup of tea before they found a mutually convenient date.

May 5, 1634
Badenburg

As was custom, they were married at the church door with the public square filled with witnesses. The fight between Karen Smith Reading's Bridal Shop in Grantville and Bruno Schroeder in Badenburg was just one more skirmish in their never-ending war over what the styles in the new timeline should be.

To Karen Reading, a purple tux was over the line for the groom, though possibly acceptable in the groomsmen—if the bridesmaids' dresses coordinated. To Bruno, any tux, even in a neon purple, was hopelessly boring. He wanted the groom looking like a peacock. David had suffered through it at Karl's and his mother's wedding, and Johan had laughed through the whole procedure. Now it was David's revenge. Even the fact that, as best man, he would be dressed in almost as much lace and embroidery as the groom didn't stop him.

Darlene laughed out loud every time she saw either of them, and then made Johan accept every flourish Bruno added.

Looking at the bills, Darlene's father made the comment that the purpose of the Baroque style was to make fathers go broke. He said that in spite of the fact that he wasn't actually being asked to pay for the wedding. Johan was quietly paying the bills.

"Well, that's over," David said, after the bride and groom made their escape. They would be spending two weeks in Magdeburg.

"A lot you know," groused Brent Partow. "We have two weeks of Grete's cooking to face. Her pepperoni rolls taste like knackwurst."

Chapter 8 — Changes and Reverses

June, 1634
Higgins Hotel

The phone in the room rang and Darlene reached for it. "Yes?"

"Good morning, ma'am. It's your wake-up call."

Darlene looked blearily at the clock. "It can't be six already. I just got to sleep." Then, blinking, she saw the clock. It was, in fact, six AM.

After looking at her, Johan rolled over and went back to sleep.

Resisting the temptation to poke him, Darlene got up and headed for the shower. Breakfast at the Twinlo Palace started at seven, and though Grete handled it, Darlene liked to be there when they opened. Which meant she had just forty minutes to shower, dress, and catch the shuttle.

There was an expression that struck Darlene, "He's so rich that his servants have servants." And in the case of David Bartley, it was the next best thing to true. She and Johan lived in the Higgins Hotel, one floor down from the penthouse. They had a suite and the staff of the hotel did the cleaning. Every day there were fresh towels, and Johan would probably get breakfast from the hotel dining room. All the while insisting that he was just Young Master David's manservant.

But he wasn't, damn it! He was a major executive in dozens of companies. He always had a briefcase full of work, and he had a secretary of his own. She shook off the thought and went about getting ready, then took the elevator down.

"Morning, Georg," she said to the elevator boy.

"Morning, ma'am," Georg said.

He was seventeen and would be going off to high school after he finished his morning shift. "They're holding the shuttle."

The shuttle was a mini-van converted to use natural gas, with a trailer attached, and it would go by Twinlo Park on its way to Badenburg, where it would turn around and come back.

"What? Why?"

"Because Frau Higgins told them to." Georg seemed confused by the question. Of course the shuttle was held for important people. But Darlene didn't think of herself as an important person.

The shuttle was a bit late, and Grete had already opened the doors of the Palace when Darlene got there. Darlene decided that, in the future, she would either have her wake up call earlier or leave breakfast in Grete's hands.

∞ ∞ ∞

Johan got his own wake-up call an hour later. He got up, got dressed and went down to have breakfast in the dining room rather than ordering room service.

"I'll have oatmeal with strawberries, Mary," he said before he got to his table. As he sat down, a lad from the newsstand came in carrying a copy of the *Daily News* and the *Grantville Times*. He ate and read the papers. Johan liked the *News* more than the *Times*. It was more fun. Breakfast finished, he looked over his appointment sheet.

He had a meeting with Kaspar about the projects that they had started in Amsterdam. At noon he had lunch scheduled with Heidi Partow, who wanted to discuss something.

She hadn't said what it was about, but it probably had to do with Adolph Schmidt's steam engine factory. And Adolph had sent Heidi, the one up-timer who worked for him, to get Johan's support for whatever it was. Johan owned about three percent of the stock in Schmidt Steam, but he was on the board as young Master David's—well, the whole Sewing Circle's—representative. And between them and the other people who Sarah or David had put into Schmidt Steam, sometimes without even mentioning it—people like Gretchen Richter, Jeff Higgins, Delia Higgins, and Dave Marcantonio—who gave the Sewing Circle their proxies, Johan voted thirty-nine percent of the stock. Add in Adolph's twenty percent and it meant that if Heidi convinced Johan, it was going to happen.

He looked forward to dinner out at Twinlo with Darlene.

September, 1634
Kipper Suite, Higgins Hotel

For the next few months, things went along swimmingly. Darlene had her new job at Twinlo Park and spent time consulting on electronic devices and working up menus. More of the latter than the former, but she was at least useful in the development of several machines that would make switch and gauge parts. And Johan was busy handling details of the expanding interests of OPM.

"You guys seem to be involved in everything," Darlene told Johan one evening when the servants had left them with a plate of cheeses and a bottle of wine and gone off to bed.

"Not really," Johan disagreed, rubbing her back with a lazy hand. "There is a great deal to be involved in. More, I think, than the most optimistic up-timer would have thought possible right after the Ring of Fire."

"I don't know what happened," Darlene complained. "It's as if the first couple of years after the Ring of Fire went by in sort of a daze for me. It seems like yesterday that the Emergency Committee was screaming about there not being enough up-timers to do all the things that absolutely had to get done. And now there is this industrial complex, and even more industry in Magdeburg."

"Well, you see, us down-timers can do some stuff," Johan said. "If you up-timers show us how."

"It doesn't seem to take a lot of showing how," she told him.

Darlene felt Johan shaking his head. "More than you might think. First time I saw a gas range, I nearly crossed myself, and me a Calvinist at the time. We need you to show us subtler stuff too, I think. It's a hard cruel world we were born into and we never learned the gentler ways of you up-timers. Still haven't, to my mind. In Amsterdam and Antwerp, they were still trying to get over on each other."

He stopped and Darlene looked back at him. "What?"

"Well, you up-timers have higher standards of decency than down-timers do."

Darlene snorted. "Bull! You should see some of the crooks we had up-time."

"Maybe," Johan said, though not like he really believed it. "But look at the way people talk about the Prince."

"Mike Stearns is not a prince, Johan. He's a two-fisted politician and like any politician, he'd sell his mother for a few votes." Darlene had a pretty jaundiced view of politics, and the election fight between Mike Stearns and Admiral Simpson had not improved that view. She'd supported Stearns, but not because she loved him. She'd supported him because she didn't want a President Pink Slip. Especially as the power plant where she had worked was owned by the government. But she had found a lot of the things Stearns said about Simpson's positions way over the top. And she hadn't been really impressed by any of them. Granted, Stearns had done okay since, even if he was way too willing to give over sovereignty to the kings and potentates of the here and now. "Not that Simpson wasn't worse. And I admit I don't really trust most of the down-time nobles as far as I could throw them. Even Gustav Adolf, and he seems the best of the lot. But it's a really bad lot."

"That's what I mean. The best of ours is not quite so good as the worst of yours."

"Now, that's not what I meant and you know it, Johan." Darlene shot Johan a hard look. "I'd rather see you as president than a lot of up-timers. Heck, I'd much rather see you as president than Simpson."

Johan turned a rather blotchy shade of red and Darlene noted, not for the first time, that blush was not **his** best color. Though making him blush was kind of fun.

November, 1634
David Bartley's Office, Other People's Money

David was getting more and more frustrated. Sarah had gone off to Magdeburg to work with the USE Federal Reserve. The name was a concession to the down-timer prejudice in favor of up-timer monetary policy. The twins were doing what they loved, and David's days were turning into a round of paperwork followed by more paperwork . . . and then for a change, still more paperwork. About the only time he got out of the office was to go to school or to do Guard drill one weekend a month. And he was getting tired of the whole mess. Not that he knew what he wanted to do instead.

He looked up as the door opened and Johan came in. "What's wrong?"

"I'm not sure, Master David," Johan said. "Darlene had an upset stomach this morning, and you know in this world any disease is dangerous. Even if Darlene says it's nothing."

"Have you called a doctor?" David asked. There were now several marginally qualified doctors in Grantville, mostly down-timers who had studied with Nichols, Adams or Shipley long enough to get the basics of modern medicine. It wasn't the same thing as having an up-time doctor, but the up-time doctors were booked solid.

"She said not to worry about it."

"Well, that's up to you. I have no understanding of women," David said.

"Sarah is just young yet," Johan said, "not ready to settle down."

"Not with me, anyway," David agreed, then shook it off. "So, what is the status of the spark plug company?" He was talking about the one that OPM was invested in, not the other one.

"More problems with expansion," Johan said, "but they are getting better and are usable, though there is some loss of pressure."

"Sometimes I think the steam heads are right and we never should have switched over to internal combustion," David complained, and they went on with the day's work.

November, 1634
Doctor's Office

Darlene missed pregnancy strips as she sat in the waiting room. They were back to the primitive days of rabbits being sacrificed to the gods of pregnancy. She knew that the developing chemical industry was trying to make strips but the specifics of how they worked and where they got the chemical reagents were a bit sketchy.

In any case, Darlene was almost sure she was pregnant, even without the test. She had been through this before, after all. She wondered how

Johan was going to react. At least money wasn't much of an issue. Johan brought in over a hundred thousand a year and Darlene herself made over fifty thousand at Twinlo Park.

Darlene had so many reasons for joy and so many reasons to fret that she was caught between the two emotions. She was thrilled to be having a new baby and terrified about the lack of up-time obstetrics. She was happy to bring a new life into the world and, at the same time, afraid of using the baby as a replacement for little Johnny. She never wanted this new life growing inside of her to wonder if it was just a replacement for what she had lost in the Ring of Fire. And she didn't want Johan to feel that way either. At the same time, she was afraid of losing the memory of the husband and son she had left up-time. That fear, she thought, was what more than anything had made adjusting to this new world so hard. As though finding happiness here would be a betrayal of her life before.

She was distracted all that day at work, and all the next day as well. Finally, she got the news. The mouse had been sacrificed in her service, and its ovaries indicated that she was pregnant. Now all she had to do was tell Johan.

November, 1634
Kipper Suite, Higgins Hotel

"You are?"

"Yes, I am."

"This . . . this is wonderful, Darlene! I never thought . . ."

"It's not like you don't have the equipment." Darlene grinned. The buttons on Johan's shirt just might pop off if he swelled with pride just a little more.

November, 1634
David Bartley's Office

"Well, congratulations, Papa." David grinned. "I'm sure you're looking forward to the changing of diapers."

Which Johan thought was a bit mean-spirited. "We will have the staff at the Higgins for that."

"Have you considered getting a place in the country? I know quite a few folks have." That included several of the newly rich up-timers and the newly rich down-timers who had appeared since the Ring of Fire. Having a home built out in the country, mostly ten or twenty miles from the Ring of Fire, where you could go to get away from the hustle and bustle of the city was popular. But there was also the factor that there were a lot of down-timers looking for work. And for a lot of the newly rich, there was increasingly a feeling of guilt about not having servants when you could afford them and they really needed the job.

If you lived in the Higgins, it wasn't an issue. There was a servant for every four guests in the Higgins. And with the way that labor-saving devices had been worked out, that was more than plenty. But using the washing machine and the vacuum cleaner yourself when there were hungry people looking for work started making you feel like Ebenezer Scrooge.

November, 1634
Kipper Suite, Higgins Hotel

"We should probably start interviewing wet nurses ahead of time," Johan said casually that evening.

"What?"

"Not all the time. I know you will want to nurse the little tyke, but are you going to want to get up at three in the morning to do it? And nursing isn't all that a wet nurse does. There is the business at the other end. I wonder, what did you up-timers do to handle that part?"

"We share the responsibility is what we do! Fathers help with the baby's care, even if they can't nurse. And we had bottles that could be filled with the milk, so that fathers could help feed the baby too."

Johan started getting a little pale as this recitation of fatherly duties flowed over him. It wasn't that he didn't already love the little thing growing in Darlene and want what was best for it. It was more that he was pretty much convinced an old soldier was anything but what was best for it. "Shouldn't we hire someone who knows something about it? It doesn't seem to me that we should risk our baby in the hands of a rank amateur."

"To start with, I've done this before."

"But I haven't!"

"You're gonna learn, dammit!"

"Yes, dear." Johan knew when to make a tactical retreat. But just in case, he was going to ask around about available wet nurses. Meanwhile, he needed to get Darlene talking to some of the other women who had recently given birth. Maybe they could talk some sense into her.

December, 1634
David Bartley's Office

"David," Franz Kunze said, "the board has decided that we will be investing more in the rail lines."

David had been afraid of that. He didn't approve. "Railroads are simply too damned expensive to be a good investment, Herr Kunze, and you know it."

"Yes, I do. But there are politics involved, and you know that. Both the government of the State of Thuringia-Franconia and the USE are pushing the railroads hard, and if we don't invest in them they have ways of making our lives difficult. Besides, the investment will eventually pay for itself."

"I'm not convinced of that, not when it's going to be competing with regular roads where the trucking company doesn't have to pay for the road. Not when it's competing with airplanes and balloons of one sort and another, which also don't have to build hundreds of miles of steel track with costs measured in the millions of dollars." This had not been an easy conclusion for David to reach. He was as fond of railroads and the romance of the rails as the next guy. But he ran the numbers, then ran the numbers again. Railroads were good for business in general, but that didn't make them a good business to be in. And David and the board had a responsibility to their investors. The railroad investments were going to be a net loss for the next several years. Eventually they might get most of their money back. They might even make a small profit, on the order of one or two percent a year. That loss would be hidden among the profits from other ventures and the average investor would never realize how much of their investment was being used to buy political favors for the board members of OPM.

"I could go public," David said, but he knew he wouldn't and so did Herr Kunze.

"No, David, you won't do that because it would do nothing but damage OPM and make you a great many enemies, both in the government and in the business community. Besides, I can make a case that OPM is invested in enough other businesses that will benefit from the cheaper transport that rails provide so that even the loss we will take on the railroads themselves will be made up for by the extra profits in our other businesses."

"Maybe," David said. "Eventually. But I can't stand by and let it happen. And it's not just the railroads. Some of the other ventures we have gotten into since I got back from Amsterdam . . ."

"Have had more to do with protecting or profiting the board than profiting the shareholders. I know. You have talked about it before. But they *are* profiting the shareholders. Profiting them greatly. The price of a share of OPM will go up by over ten percent this year."

"But it could have gone up fifteen. Perhaps twenty."

"Possibly. But you know by now how business gets done."

David looked at this man who had been one of his mentors since before the founding of OPM. "Yes, I do, sir. But it's getting a bit hard to take."

"Then don't take it," Franz Kunze said. "Look, David. You are a young man forced by circumstance into your current role. Don't misunderstand me. You fulfill that role admirably. But, for now, it might be best if you took a leave of absence from the job of CEO of OPM. Go do something else. Take the grand tour, as is custom for young men of your station in life."

"Am I being fired?"

"No, you are not being fired. If you choose to stay, you will be expected to support and implement the board's decision on the railroads and on many other decisions that you disagree with. David, you need a break. I won't make you take it, but I do recommend it."

"I'll think about it, sir."

December, 1634
Higgins Penthouse, Higgins Hotel

"What am I going to do?" David asked his grandmother as he plopped down onto the chair in the greenhouse. The roof of the Higgins Hotel had a greenhouse with south-facing windows, and in winter Delia Higgins liked to sit out here, looking out at the Ring Wall and smelling the summer flowers that she could grow only because of the greenhouse.

Johan stood by the door, but by now David knew that telling him to sit down would do no good.

"What do you want to do?" Delia said. "I'd hire you, but I think you'll be bored silly. Besides, I'd have to make up a job for you. Mary is handling the hotel quite well, and Karl is handling the warehouse. You want to be my investment counselor?"

David held up his hands, as though pushing the idea away. "Probably not a good idea, Grandma," he said, remembering the fight over the Higgins Hotel.

"Go into the army?" Delia offered as a thought. "Your grandpaw served, your father's stationed in Magdeburg right now. Besides you were in Junior ROTC all the way through high school, and I know it's not West Point or anything, but you took the classes and did all right in them. There's a good chance you could get a commission."

Johan was looking utterly shocked at this suggestion, and David found himself grinning. "What do you think, Johan?"

"I think it's the craziest thing I have heard Frau Higgins ever say, and I've heard her say a lot of crazy things over the last three years."

"Starting with 'you're hired,' " Delia Higgins said.

"Yes, that would be the first one," Johan agreed easily. "Hire a former mercenary to guard a fortune in goods. Like I said, crazy. But not as crazy as having young Master David waste his time in the army."

"Why not?" David asked. "If it was good enough for Don Fernando, the Cardinal-Infante of Spain, why isn't it good enough for a poor West Virginia boy who got a little lucky in the market?"

"Don Fernando couldn't have started a sewing machine company."

"I don't think that lack keeps him up nights." David laughed.

"Probably not, but the Cardinal-Infante was raised to be a soldier."

"And I have had four years of Junior ROTC," David said. "I have as good a military education as half the officers serving in the army right now."

Johan winced visibly. "In a way, you have more military education than ninety percent of them. But in another way, you're as green as any recruit I have ever seen. All your knowledge is book learning. And that's a dangerous mix."

"I've been in the National Guard for almost six months. More, if you include the time that the Junior ROTC spent training with the guard."

Johan winced again. "Yes. You have done drill and dress ranks. You have learned to march and salute, and even dig a fox hole. But you have never killed a man or stood in line while hundreds of men tried to kill you."

David felt his mouth firming. He knew that Johan was right, but at the same time Johan was also wrong. He didn't know how he would react in combat, but no one did till they got there. And he did have the book learning.

Besides, armies needed support staff. They needed logistics. He had been disappointed when, even before the trip to Amsterdam, the National Guard had accepted him and assigned him to supply. He had been especially upset when he realized it was so they could use his connections to get better gear cheaper. But he had dug in, and the Grantville High School unit of the State of Thuringia-Franconia National Guard had indeed ended up with good equipment.

"I think I will look into it," David said.

"Not without me, you won't, young Master David."

"I quite agree, assuming the army will allow it," Delia said.

"Really? How do you think Darlene is going to react?"

December, 1634
Kipper Suite, Higgins Hotel

"You're going to do fucking what? Are you out of your mind?" Darlene's face was red and getting more so.

"I have a duty."

"What duty?" She waved her arms.

"I . . ." Johan stopped and tried to think how he could explain to his up-timer wife in a way she would understand. "When I was hungry, they took me in. I was a stranger, and they took me in. The Bible says that in Matthew . . . or something very like it. But it's really true with David and his grandmother. I was a stranger and they invited me in, gave me a place. David is a good boy, well on his way to being a man. But he has very little experience in military matters. He needs someone to look after him and see that he stays out of trouble. And that's my job. It's been my job since the day Delia Higgins took in a stranger to guard the family and look out for them in dealing with down-timers."

"But, Johan, what about your responsibility—your *duty*—to me and the baby I'm carrying? Don't we count at all? You're going to go off to war and leave us behind, to follow someone who doesn't need you the way we do!"

"Now, don't you be overstating the thing. David's probably going to be stationed right here in Grantville. He's going to see about going full-time in the National Guard of the State of Thuringia-Franconia, not the USE Army. I'll be home most nights and well . . ." Johan managed to stop before adding, "it means I can avoid changing diapers."

Darlene wasn't exactly thrilled, but Johan made a good case that one, it was his duty and two, it wasn't going to be that bad.

Chapter 9 — A Man in Uniform

January 7, 1635
National Guard Camp, Outside Saalfeld

Johan, in his entire military career, had never worn a uniform of this quality. Truthfully, most of the time, he hadn't worn a uniform at all. But the State of Thuringia-Franconia and the USE did things differently, or at least they were starting to.

Johan hadn't lied to Darlene when he said that David was going into the Guard, not the regular army. Not exactly. . . . Partly it was because the way the up-timers managed things like chain of command was an odd mix of up-time, down-time, and new-time procedures. In the case of the State of Thuringia-Franconia, the permanent duty National Guard were actually in the national army of the USE. They were just assigned to the guard units.

On the other hand, Johan was officially a military auxiliary, not in the regular army per se, which was how the USE Army had decided to treat the personnel hired privately by officers as their servants and batmen. To the best of Johan's knowledge, he was the only person of that status who was hired by an up-timer, but he might well be wrong about that. It didn't affect his fancy new uniform, except for the special patch on his right shoulder that indicated his "outside the normal chain of command" status.

Johan loved his dress blues and he was even pleased with the working greens. Having both dress and undress uniforms was a luxury which affected his first sight of Major Tandy Walker in blue jeans and a shirt and jacket with rank insignia pinned to its collar. Surely the man could do better than that for a uniform!

Johan announced them, and the sergeant behind the desk said, "Through that door" without looking up from the book he was reading.

Johan opened the door and followed Master David in. Then he got his first look at Major Tandy Walker. Major Walker was a heavyset man in the prime of life, and the natural question that first occurred to Johan seeing him was: how did a man who was the son of the head of the USE Federal Reserve end up as a base commander of a minor base in the State of Thuringia-Franconia National Guard? It wasn't a question in this case, though, because Johan already knew the answer.

Tandy Walker was as prickly as his father and even more straitlaced. He offended people, important people. He was good at the mechanics of the job, but he maintained a belief that all down-timers were thieves and ignorant of civilized behavior. He took offense at the tilt of a hat and gave it back just as quickly.

Johan stood in the background, a silent witness and also a reminder—if the uniforms weren't enough—of just how wealthy young Master David was. Johan tended to respect up-timers perhaps a little more than he should. But, in a way, people like Tandy Walker were part of the reason why. A down-timer might well be just as much of a prick, but he would be trying to prove how important he was, not how honorable.

The major had clearly not used the post of commandant to his advantage.

Supply Depot

A few hours later, Johan had one arm thrown over the shoulder of Sergeant-soon-to-be-Corporal Franz Beckmann, smiling genially as he explained the new circumstances. Johan had known a hundred Beckmanns in his life. Some had had power over him, and a few he had had power over. They were what the army required, but they needed someone sharp to watch them.

That would be Johan's job, while young Master David came up with ways to make this little corner of the army work better.

National Guard Camp

"What do you think, Johan?" David asked, after they'd left Beckmann's domain.

"That depends, sir." Since they were in the army, Johan was calling young Master David sir, which was military protocol and didn't make the young master quite so uncomfortable. "Do you want to ruin Major Walker and send Beckmann to prison?"

"Not particularly," David said. "In fact, I would like to avoid both those outcomes. If we can do so without too much cost."

"It may cost a bit. Beckmann has been systematically looting the place. I'm sure of that, but it will take a while to figure out just how."

"What will you need?"

"A couple of clerks. I'll take care of it."

January 8, 1635
Supply Depot

Beckmann spent the first night after Lieutenant Bartley's arrival sweating bullets. Then Johan Kipper returned the next morning, and his worst fears proved insufficient to the occasion. Johan had a pair of clerks with him to do a careful item-by-item check of the contents of the warehouse.

"What happens now, Sergeant Kipper?" Beckmann asked after the clerks got down to it.

"That mostly depends on what you did with the money," Johan said.

"I can cut you in, Sergeant," Beckmann offered desperately, and the sergeant actually laughed.

"Do you know how much I made last year, Franz? Never mind. It's none of your business, anyway. You're small potatoes, as the up-timers would say."

"Then what?"

"That will be up to the lieutenant. We are going to put everything back, Franz. And what we're short of will come out of your hide."

At that point, Franz Beckmann made the biggest mistake of his life. He sighed in relief.

Johan Kipper laughed.

January 10, 1635
Kipper Suite, Higgins Hotel

Darlene did like a man in uniform. At least, *this* man in uniform. Also, in a way, Johan seemed happier. He had been a soldier for a very long time, and even if the army was different, it was more the sort of job he was used to. Besides, half Johan's reason for being there was to keep David out of combat and that would entail keeping Johan out of combat too.

Every morning Johan got up, got dressed, and joined David as they headed off to the camp. The conversations weren't even all that different. Logistics and supply are logistics and supply, whether you're dealing with military or business.

January 12, 1635
Higgins Hotel, Dining Room

"Captain Ponte's company has been released," Johan said one morning. Darlene had given up going to Twinlo for breakfast, instead opting to sleep a little later and have breakfast with Johan and, often, David.

"When did you hear?" David Bartley asked, as he had a sip of apple juice. Unlike Johan's bowl of oatmeal, David had a plate piled high with eggs, bacon, and sausages, and a bowl of apples.

"Karl called me last night."

"Do you think they will go for it?"

"Who will go for what?" Darlene asked. This was a new one.

"Ponte is a mercenary captain in the service of Gustav Adolf," Johan told her. "He has a small infantry company, about two hundred men and their dependents. Mostly halberds, only about sixty musketeers. They aren't a bad company, but not first line troops either. And Gustav has informed them that they are no longer needed. Not with all the CoC-raised regiments."

"Are they friends of yours?"

"Karl is," Johan said, "but though I know a few more of them, Karl is my only real friend in the company."

"Then why the interest? Is this Karl looking for a job? And, by the way, do the Germans have any other names besides Karl?"

"Of course they do, dear," Johan said. "There's Big Karl, little Karl, Squinty-eyed Karl, lots of different names."

"I believe that they also have the name Hans. I'm not sure there is a third," David offered with a grin. "I think that this Karl is actually Dutch, though. Someone you met when you first went in the army, back in the Netherlands?"

125

"Yes. Karl Aalders. He joined about three years after I did and I introduced him to army life when I still thought it was glorious. It took me awhile to realize that we were just paid killers."

There was a world of regret in that sentence, and David cleared his throat. "Karl Aalders got in touch with Johan six months ago,

wondering if he was the same Johan Kipper and it turned out he was. It seemed that Ponte was starting to worry about his company's future and didn't want to work for the Hapsburgs."

"Not didn't want to. Couldn't," Johan corrected. "There was some sort of a scandal. Karl insists that it wasn't Ponte's fault. The girl liked his looks and things got out of hand."

David snorted. "I met Giuseppe Ponte last month in Magdeburg. Wavy black hair with gray wings at the temples. I bet the girl did like his looks. Even Sarah took a second look at him, then talked about his 'Latin flair.' To me he just seemed like he was a bit full of himself."

"According to Karl, he cares about his troops and their families," Johan said.

"Yes, I think he does. That's why I'm considering it. He is a Roman Catholic who commands a troop of Lutherans and Calvinists and they all seem to get along pretty well. Well enough that they want to stay together."

"Karl was looking to get hired as a company to act as guards for the various Higgins' enterprises. We didn't have enough guard positions for a company half that size, and most of the ones we did have were already filled. But I said I would look into it and see if I could find anything.

"About that time, I had my little argument with the board of directors and Giuseppe Ponte offered to sell me his company and stay on as my executive and training officer, so that if I should choose to go into the army, I would do so with a rank commensurate to my station. And he was hoping that with me buying the company and equipping them with modern weapons, they wouldn't be deactivated." David took another sip of juice.

"That's actually pretty clever," Darlene said. "Of course, if you had taken Johan off to Magdeburg, I would have had you assassinated."

David gulped theatrically, then grinned at her. "Yes, it was clever and I was almost tempted. But I have no desire to be a mercenary captain. What did occur to me was that a military company might make a cohesive work force for other projects. I suggested that to Captain Ponte, but he still wanted to have his rank."

"I can sort of understand that. He has invested everything he owns into the company and he doesn't have anyplace else to go," Johan said.

"That's sad," Darlene said.

"Yes, but I'm not sure if I can get him to see reason, even now."

"Perhaps you won't have to," Johan said.

"What do you mean?"

"Well, you're in the regular army, but assigned to the State of Thuringia-Franconia National Guard. What about getting their company into the National Guard?"

"Won't pay the bills. A weekend a month simply won't pay his people enough to get by on."

"But it will let the captain keep his rank. And if we find regular work for them the rest of the time . . ."

"Doing what?"

"You were talking about needing uniforms," Darlene said. "Why not set up a ready-to-wear clothing factory and make uniforms for the State of Thuringia-Franconia National Guard?"

"That's a good idea," David said, cautiously. "I'm not sure that the State of Thuringia-Franconia Guard would be enough of a customer, but we might be able to get extra contracts."

"Why don't you call your friend and see what he thinks?"

January 15, 1635
Supply Depot

For a week the clerks and Johan Kipper went over Beckmann's books and the contents of the warehouse. Then came the return of David Bartley.

∞ ∞ ∞

"Time to call the cops?" Johan asked, and Franz Beckmann swallowed.

"Not just yet," David said. "Sergeant Beckmann strikes me as a saving sort of fellow. Not the type to blow his ill-gotten gains on wild women and drink."

Johan looked over at the sweating sergeant. "Could be. Not that it matters. After he's arrested, they will seize his assets."

The icy blue eyes of Lieutenant David Bartley turned on Franz, and any thought that Beckmann might have had that the up-timer was soft disappeared.

"Tell me, Sergeant Beckmann," the cold-eyed young man asked, "do you invest in the stock market?" A very short pause as the eyes locked onto his, "Yes, I can see that you do. You know, Sergeant, they keep quite good records of stock transactions, with computers. Brokers record who they were buying stock from and for. It's not nearly as good a place to hide money as most people seem to think . . ."

Franz Beckmann knew he was trapped, but the officer was still talking.

"There are three options open to you, Sergeant. First is: if you don't cooperate, you are arrested, the forensic accountants go over your books and dig out every dime you have stolen and every dime that you have made from investing your ill-gotten gains, and seize the whole works. Then you go to prison and come out in several years a poorer but, hopefully, wiser man."

"Option two: come clean with me, make good the missing gear in the form of cash and stocks of equivalent value and a fine to go into company funds. Accept company punishment. You will certainly lose a stripe."

"What's the third option?" Franze asked. He had to know.

And the young man winced in mock sympathy. "The third option is if you try to fake us out. If you pretend to cooperate, but keep some back."

"What happens then?"

"I let Johan deal with that."

Behind David Bartley, Johan Kipper smiled, showing perfect false teeth in a perfect false smile in a worn and damaged face. And his eyes were even colder than David Bartley's icy blue ones.

Sergeant Beckmann looked into those two sets of eyes. He was good at reading people and he thought there was a chance that David Bartley was bluffing. That Bartley might not catch him if he hid just a bit for himself. Then he looked into Johan Kipper's eyes . . . and chose option two.

Sergeant Beckmann sold his entire portfolio for one dollar and other valuable considerations. Part of those other valuable considerations was keeping from going to jail. But on the upside, Lieutenant Bartley would sign off on the original set of books and pay for the replacement of the missing goods out of his own pocket. The rest of the money he'd earned in the stock market would pay his fine to the company and then go toward the uniforms that the State of Thuringia-Franconia reserves would need.

January 20, 1635
Gorndorf

"Well, Captain Ponte, how do you like Gorndorf?" Johan asked.

"It's a village. I know that your Signor Bartley is planning improvements, and the women like the idea of having their own gardens, but we are not farmers."

"I know. Most of the fields are going to be rented to up-time farmers, though we are keeping enough for some gardens. No, this is going to be a company town. There will be a clothing factory where the sewing machines and pattern tables and cutting tools are set up. The idea will be to produce good clothing very cheaply."

"I know. Signor Bartley explained about the uniforms and the civilian wear you are hoping to make. It's just not what I was hoping for."

"One weekend a month you will be training, and Lieutenant Bartley approves of one day a week of extra training. The company will stay in good form."

"One day a week and one weekend a month is nothing like enough training to keep them sharp. It's barely enough to keep the rust off."

Which Johan knew was true, but these were to be National Guard troops, not regulars. If they got called up, they would have some warning. And they were already an experienced company. They wouldn't break, not after what most of them had seen. Besides . . . "You and your officers and sergeants get to keep your rank. It's just in the State of Thuringia-Franconia National Guard now. With the income from the clothing company, you will be making as much as you were as a mercenary company." Johan didn't lose his patience, but it was getting a little frayed. "Captain Ponte, you have received a stroke of great good fortune, one that allows you to stay with your company and allows them to make a living. And even to keep their military honors. Don't blow that good fortune by whining that everything is not just as you would prefer."

Ponte looked at Johan and sighed. "I know, Sergeant Kipper. I do know. It's just hard."

January 20, 1635
Supply Depot

"So, how is he taking it?" David asked.

Johan knew that David let him handle Captain Ponte because of David's youth and Johan's military experience. There were a number of things that the haughty Italian captain would take from an old soldier that he wouldn't from a stripling youth, no matter that it was the stripling who was paying the bills. "He'll get over it. And the company is settling in well enough. The hemp mix fabrics are strong and not uncomfortable, and the women have gotten used to the sewing machines."

"What about guns?"

"We will be using the SRG."

"I hate that. Especially

considering the French Cardinal rifles. I don't like our people being out-gunned."

"Neither do I, sir, but this is a second-line unit. The new rifles are going to the regular army and they don't have enough."

David grunted.

January 25, 1635
Kipper Suite, Higgins Hotel

"Do you really think that David Bartley is right about Saxony attacking us here?" Darlene asked Johan late one evening. They had just finished having supper in their suite and were snuggling on the couch.

"No."

"Then why?"

"Because it's much better to be prepared for what doesn't happen than to be unprepared for what does. And, besides, it keeps the boy busy and productive. You do realize that Ponte Clothing is going to turn a nice profit? Most of that profit isn't going to come from the uniform sales to the guard. It's going to come from Wishbook sales."

"How does that work?" Darlene asked.

"We put together the factory to get the uniforms, but once it was in place the fixed costs were already taken care of and the factory and workers were there. So we turn out simple, solid, basic clothing at a fraction of the cost that a tailor could charge. The clothing we sell will be the first set of new clothing that most of our customers will ever have owned. Most of them will have spent their lives never once buying a new pair of pants. Now they can, and for not that much more than used or twice-used clothing would have cost them before."

"I guess we really are making a difference. Sometimes it doesn't seem like it, but I guess we are."

"A lot of people are going to avoid frostbite because of our winter clothing line this year. David remembered seeing pictures of something called a *telogreika*, a Russian winter jacket and pants. He talked to Bruno, and they worked out a design. If we have to fight a war in the winter, our people will be warm. And if we don't, a lot of farmers will still be warm."

"What do the twins have you working on?"

"Brushes for generators, and we have a new recipe for General Tso's chicken." Darlene grinned. "I'm not sure if it tastes like the real thing, but then again, I'm not sure that what I had in West Virginia up-time tasted like the Chinese version, so who cares. It tastes good and the customers like it."

Chapter 10 — In the Real Army Now

June 6, 1635
Twinlo Palace, Twinlo Park

avid approached the private booth in the restaurant at Twinlo park. "I'm being transferred." He tried manfully to hide his smile as he added, "I'm to be on General Stearns' staff in the Third Division."

Darlene was having no difficulty suppressing a smile. She doubted if she could call one up if her life depended on it. And the fact that she was eight months pregnant, looked like a whale, and was sure that Johan would follow the little creep into the regular army didn't help.

But she didn't say anything. Now was not the time.

June 6, 1635
Kipper Suite, Higgins Hotel

"You are *not* going," Darlene said. "I'm about to have a baby, and I need you here."

Johan looked at his beautiful, much younger wife and was very tempted to stay right here. No one could make him go. Young Master David wouldn't even ask him to go.

But "on the general's staff" wasn't all that safe a place to be in the seventeenth century. Johan knew that perfectly well, having grown up and lived his life in a world where generals and their staffs led cavalry charges.

He remembered the day he had arrived and the discussion that he and the then fourteen-year-old David Bartley had. Up-timers were good people, but they needed taking care of, and Darlene would be right here in Grantville with the best doctors and support in the world.

David, on the other hand, would be out on what Frank Jackson called "the sharp end." Johan had to go, much as he didn't want to. For Darlene's sake, Johan had to do this. But how could he explain it to her . . . ?

He took a breath to steady himself and said, "In all the time I served in the armies that fought across Europe from the time I was fifteen, I never fought for a cause. I fought for the money. It was just a job. David is going to fight for the USE. And even if we end up fighting Poland after we take out Saxony, the USE is still something worth fighting for. And the sort of serfdom they have in Poland is something worth fighting against."

"Dammit, Johan! You're going because the so-called emperor is pissed off at his brother-in-law. That's *all* this is about. Gustav doesn't have as much territory as he wants. He never *will* have as much as he wants. What's next? Russia?"

"No. I'm going because the USE is involved. And for that matter, the emperor has every right to be more than annoyed with his brother-in-law and with John George of Saxony. I haven't studied as much of your up-timer history as young Master David has, but the Junior ROTC course spent quite a bit of time on your American Civil War. When the southern states seceded, what would have happened to America if the North had let them go? That has been a major topic of discussion since Saxony and Brandenburg effectively seceded from the USE."

"I heard something about that argument." Darlene sat back in her chair. "But I don't remember them coming to any conclusion."

"That's because getting a couple of Civil War buffs to agree on what color uniforms were worn by the blue and the gray is the next best thing to impossible. But what David thinks and what I think after listening to them argue is that once the precedent of secession was established, it wouldn't have stopped either in the north or the south. States would have seceded over anything from fishing rights to how they packed a mule. And the United States would have ceased to be united in any real sense."

"That sort of makes sense, but I don't recall hearing much about that conclusion up-time."

"From what I understand, it's gained popularity, mostly since Saxony and Brandenburg seceded, so you wouldn't have. But what people are afraid of, at least what David and I are afraid of, is that if Gustav decides to be conciliatory and let Saxony and Brandenburg go, it will spell the end of the USE. Not this year, and probably not next, but other provinces will start seceding or threatening to secede any time the crown or central government does anything they don't like. It wouldn't take much of that to end the USE before it got going."

"Fine," she said, just as annoyed as she started out. "Saxony and Brandenburg have to be forced back into the union, but why do you have to do it? Why does David Bartley have to do it, for that matter? If we were up-time, someone like David wouldn't have been drafted. Not in Vietnam, not even in WWII. They would have taken one look and said 'deferred to vital civilian occupation.' "

"David was fourteen at the Battle of the Crapper. Fifteen at the Battle of Jena and when he stood on the bleachers in the high school gym while Jeff Higgins and Vice Principal Len Trout stood against the Croats," Johan told her. "The West Virginia tradition of service is not dead in the down-time world and, well, I don't think David could live with himself if he sat back getting rich while others did the dying." Johan reached out and took Darlene's hand. "Darlene, when the kids started HSMC, it wasn't because they were trying to get rich. It was because Sarah Wendell explained to them her parent's worries about living on capital. It was done to support their families, but even more to support Grantville and the up-timers. It was all they could do to defend Grantville."

"And you?"

"They took me in and made me rich, gave me a place and opportunity. How much less of a man would you have me be than David?"

Darlene sighed. "I'm not happy about this. But I do get it. So, go if you feel you have to. But one of these days, you're going to realize that you are just as important as David Bartley. And, to me, *you* are *more* important than he is."

She struggled to stand, all eight months of pregnancy showing. "I'm going to be *really* pissed off if you get killed."

July 5, 1635
Magdeburg Navy Officer's Club

Johan followed David into the club in Magdeburg. It was actually the Navy Club because Admiral Simpson had established it. But it was quite a nice place, and the officers of the army frequented it as well. David was looking around for someone he knew but not finding anyone. Johan looked around too, and found a few familiar faces, people that he recognized from a few years earlier when for a time his unit had been serving with Gustav Adolf. But while he knew a few, none would know him. What officer is going to remember a private who paraded by them at this or that battle or review?

"It seems a bit crowded," David said, and Johan nodded. The place was packed. Magdeburg was the primary staging area for the move into Saxony and the whole city was crowded with military personnel. Any military club was going to be packed.

There was a wave from a table and David looked behind himself to see who was being waved at. No one was there. Then David headed toward the waver, who was holding an open seat for him.

"You're Bartley, aren't you?" said a major with bright orange muttonchop sideburns.

"Yes, sir. Lieutenant David Bartley."

"Thought so, Lieutenant. We may be related. I'm Major David Barclay. Not quite the same, I grant, but the spelling could have changed over the years. It was the name, though, that struck me first a few months ago when I saw it in *The Street*. So what is a member of the new capitalist class doing in the army? It's not like you're here to make your fortune like I am."

Young Master David blushed a bit, Johan noticed, but there was no noticeable hesitation. "Civic duty, I guess. Someone's got to and it might as well be me."

The major, who Johan guessed to be in his mid-twenties, gave young Master David a sharp look that turned into a more measuring look. Then he nodded. "Good answer, lad, and makes me a little ashamed of my own motives. I was here a bit to defend Protestantism, but mostly to make my fortune, as I said. And that's honestly still why I'm here."

"There's nothing wrong with making a fortune that I'm aware of, sir," David said with a smile. "If nothing else, it gives you the opportunity to do more. This is Johan Kipper, my aide."

Johan gave David a look that said, clear as if he had shouted it, that there was no reason for David to introduce him, then said, "Major," with a brief nod and a brace to not quite attention. But it wasn't really true that there was no need for an introduction, and Johan knew it. David sometimes introduced Johan to people specifically to see how they would react. It was a fairly good barometer of how they were dealing with the new rules.

Major Barclay seemed to be adjusting well enough. He simply smiled and said, "Sergeant Kipper."

"So where are you stationed, Major Barclay?" Lieutenant David Bartley asked.

"I was just transferred to Third Division. Black Falcon Regiment, commanded by Colonel Friedrich Eichelberger. I am to be their S4. Do you happen to know what an S4 is supposed to be?"

"S stands for Staff, 4 is logistics. Supply, not to put too fine a point on it."

"Well, that's good. I was in supply before and I have found I have something of a knack for it."

That wasn't, from David Bartley's point of view, an overwhelmingly good thing. The question was whether Major Barclay had a knack for making sure his unit was supplied or making sure that his pockets got lined. Of course, there was no law that said it couldn't be both. David could live with both, though Major Barclay was unlikely to find as many ways to line his pockets as in the old-style army. David took a quick look at the man. He was well—but not extravagantly—dressed and was a bit on the portly side, but not overly so. "We will probably meet sometimes. I'm assigned to Colonel McAdam, the S4 for the Third Division.

"What do you do there?"

"I don't know yet, sir. I just arrived today and will be meeting him tomorrow."

July 6, 1635
Third Division S4 outside Magdeburg

"Sir, Lieutenant Bartley reporting as ordered." Johan watched as Master David braced to attention in the up-timer fashion. The young master was in dress blues in the up-timer style as defined by the JROTC books. They were custom made by Master David's clothing company. Then he looked over at Colonel Paul McAdam. The colonel was wearing a buff coat with his clan plaid strung crossbody from right shoulder to left hip. He was seated, but behind a table, not a desk, so Johan could see he wore up-time style trousers. Not quite blue jeans, but close. If Johan was any judged—and he was—the colonel's boots were made by the Schumacher shoe factory. Probably bought through one of the catalogs.

"Ah, Lieutenant Bartley. I've heard about you."

"Good things, I hope, sir."

"Well. I suppose that would depend . . . " Colonel McAdam began, then petered off in what the colonel apparently thought was an ominous manner. Johan didn't even twitch an eyebrow. *As if he could threaten Master David so.*

"Have a seat, Lieutenant Bartley. What do you know about the supply situation?" At the colonel's gesture, Master David sat. He didn't gesture for Johan to sit, thank goodness. Now was not the time for one of Master David's experiments.

"Not as much as I would like, sir."

"Well, it's not that bad here in Magdeburg. We have the river and we're in the center of the, well, everything."

Master David nodded. In Magdeburg you could get almost anything you could get in Grantville and more of it. Magdeburg was the largest manufacturing center in the USE, and that meant in the world.

The colonel nodded back, a single, quick jerk of his head and continued. "But it's not going to be that easy once the campaign starts. Even the best army in the world can't carry enough food and fodder to keep it fed very long in the field. The canning and freeze-drying would help, but there is very little of it so far when you're talking about feeding an army instead of a few rich people. What will help some, I hope, is the Elbe as we move into Saxony. But if we end up more than a few miles from the Elbe, we're going to have to do what we've always done. *Buy* from the locals. And if the rumors are right about Poland, that's going to be even worse." There was, Johan noted, a strange emphasis on the word "buy." Perhaps as though another word would have been used if the colonel was talking to another down-timer.

"Buy?" David asked.

The colonel gave David a careful look, then another quick jerk of a nod. "That's the best we can hope for, Lieutenant. Before the Ring of Fire we would have gone through the land like locusts. But we're not supposed to do that anymore, and your job is going to be arranging to have us meet with merchants willing to sell the army food."

Johan listened as David and the colonel discussed the Third Division's budget for the campaign. Uniforms, weapons, powder, and shot would be provided by army stores here in Magdeburg. Food was going to be a bigger problem. An army, or even a division, went through a lot of food every day. Transporting that much food was the next best thing to impossible. So they were going to have to buy foodstuffs in route.

"I, ah, do have some connections in the business community, sir. I can see what sort of bargains I can find?"

"I know up-time APCs are out of the question for transport, but can you get us steam wagons?"

"Not a chance!" David shook his head. "Adolph Schmidt builds what I think are the best steam engines for the price in Magdeburg, but he's at least six months behind on orders, and the other two Magdeburg companies making steam engines are almost as far behind. The companies up in Grantville are even farther behind on orders. People are patriotic enough, but business is business, and they have contracts with people who have already paid for their steam engines.

"Between you, me, and every drover or muleskinner in Germany, a steam engine is worth at least three times the price of the equivalent number of horses—good horses, not nags halfway to the glue factory. And that's mostly what they sell for. If I go to Adolph on bended knee, I may get him to bump us up on the order list to the tune of half a dozen steam engines or so. I'm a major stockholder, after all. But even if I do, using them to power wagons would mostly be a waste since they can power factories or river boats where you get more bang for your buck."

"Even half a dozen might help," Colonel McAdam pointed out. "As I said, we're likely to be using barges to ferry supplies upriver to Saxony. At least at first."

Johan decided he would have a chat with the union rep at the Schmidt plant. The union was just about all CoC and they might be able to squeeze out a couple of extras.

"I'll see what I can do, sir," Master David said.

The colonel nodded. "Good. But you're right, half a dozen steam wagons wouldn't be enough to make much difference. Do you know how much it takes to feed, clothe and house an army?"

"I know what the books say it takes, sir," David said. "I don't know how well the books agree with the reality."

They talked requirements then, in food and equipage. The answer to how much supplies an army consumes came out to various values of "a hell of a lot" and "even more than that," now that they wouldn't be looting the countryside as they marched.

That was something that Colonel McAdam agreed was very fine and noble, but also something he wasn't convinced was practical. "I mean, if the other side is living in large part off the land and we're trailing along this monstrous logistic tail . . . it's a weak point the enemy can take advantage of." It was a problem that neither of them, nor anyone else in the Third Division's S4 section, had a solution for. Not then, anyway.

∞ ∞ ∞

Johan and David left the office of Colonel McAdam, and Master David turned to Johan. "I'm going to get out of the monkey suit and into fatigues. Why don't you go see what Major Barclay wants?"

July 6, 1635
Black Falcon Regimental Headquarters, outside
Magdeburg

"So tell me, Sergeant, how does Lieutenant Bartley do it?" Major Barclay asked after he had invited Johan to sit and offered him a small beer.

Johan had been expecting that question or one like it. The smart ones always asked him that. "In large part, it's the way he sees the world, sir. He was born up-time and spent his first few years there, but was still young enough to adapt to down-time ways and he has come to understand how things work in both worlds, so he sees how they fit. And how they don't."

"Not something that could be readily picked up?"

Now that wasn't a question Johan was expecting. "No, sir, I don't think so."

"Yet you seem to have done quite well?"

"That's different," Johan said, then stopped. "You know, sir, I think there is something else to young Master David's success. He has a talent for picking people and then letting them do what they do without interfering. No, that's not it. He smoothes the way."

"I'm not sure I understand." Major Barclay looked confused.

"I'm a pretty good bargainer, sir." Johan smiled. "Delia Higgins, David's grandmother, says I bargain like a fishwife. Whatever that means. When I am bargaining with someone and most other up-timers are there, they will explain how this or that works and it can make the bargaining difficult, but David will watch what I am doing without seeming to and back my play."

The major nodded, and Johan realized that the major had some of what David had. Or something, anyway. This wasn't the sort of conversation Johan had been expecting and he hadn't meant to let so much out. "What did you wish to discuss, Major?"

"The powder consignment is fine, but the cartridge papers are short. We are going to need those if we are going to get the cartridges made up before we march," Major Barclay said. "But that's just the official reason. My real question, Sergeant, is: do you think you could get me into some of the lieutenant's projects? The whole brigade has heard about Jeff Higgins' good luck."

"I doubt that Captain Higgins is thrilled to have the world learn he is a millionaire, sir."

"Probably not, but there is no way something like that stays secret. And in this case, there was no way that how it happened was going to remain secret, either."

Well, that was true enough, Johan thought, and if there was one thing he had learned it was that success bred success. HSMC had made OPM possible and OPM had made any number of companies possible because the money to make that initial investment was easily available. That aura of success had apparently followed young Master David into the army. Which wasn't necessarily a good thing. There were going to be people trying to get in on any deal. And some who would insist that he come up with some deal for them to get into, just as there had been back in Grantville. The fact that some of those people were going to outrank David Bartley by a considerable margin could be a real problem. At least Major Barclay was being polite about it. So far, anyway.

"I understand, Major, and I'll see what I can do. But we have only just arrived and young Master David is very busy arranging for foodstuffs to be available to Third Division as we head into Saxony."

∞ ∞ ∞

As it turned out, David Bartley had rather less contact with Major Barclay than Johan did. David was much too busy with the special assignment that Colonel McAdam had given him to do the coordinating that was his official job. That fell to Johan and Sergeant Beckmann, who had come with David at Major Walker's insistence. "I don't want your tame crook anywhere near supplies without you there to watch him," Major Walker had said in his usual acerbic way. Actually, David wished he could have brought his company, but they were strictly National Guard. Besides, they were doing quite well making clothing.

Johan, on the other hand, ended up doing most of the coordinating with the various brigade and regimental supply offices. Mostly through the supply sergeants. But not in the case of Major Barclay.

July 8, 1635
Magdeburg, Strauss Coffee House

"How do you do, Herr Krause?" David said. "I'm here to talk to you about arranging shipments of grain for Third Division." Herr Krause was a tall man and not quite gaunt. He was a merchant from Saxony and the factor who controlled the grain output from over twenty villages in Saxony. He had half a dozen barges that plied the Elbe River.

"So I gathered, Herr Bartley. What I don't understand is what David Bartley is doing pretending to be a lieutenant in the army?" Herr Krause was apparently a plain-spoken man and David responded in kind.

"Not pretending, sir. I am Lieutenant Bartley."

"That's a shame, son. I could use David Bartley, the man of affairs. Lieutenant Bartley isn't someone I would even bother to meet with."

"But Lieutenant Bartley is authorized to guarantee payment for goods delivered to the Third Division. A division has a lot of mouths to feed and needs a lot of rye."

"Sure, son." Krause waved his hand vaguely. "But what are you going to pay me with?"

"American dollars."

"You mean the new USE dollars, don't you?"

"Yes, but if you would prefer I can get you silver. Though there will be an additional charge for the trouble."

Krause snorted. "You mean they're already discounting the USE dollars, don't you, son?"

"No, sir. The surcharge for using silver goes both ways. You want to buy something and bring us silver, there is the same surcharge. We work from the most recent exchange rate on the Magdeburg market."

Krause tilted his head. "You're not bluffing, are you, boy? You really think the USE money is going to be just as good as the American dollars?"

"Yes, I do."

"What about Gustav Adolf?"

"What about him?"

"He has an army to field. He needs money. Giving him the keys to the printing house that prints money is like giving a drunk the keys to the winery."

"I know Coleman Walker, sir." David found himself grinning at the man. "It would take more than one of Gustav Adolf's armies to make him see reason. The biggest issue we are going to face is not enough money. We absolutely won't have too much."

"Huh? What do you mean?"

"Coleman Walker is a fiscal conservative, and the more he's pushed, the more conservative he gets. He didn't want to issue enough money to support the goods that we had with us in the Ring of Fire and he didn't want to issue enough money to support the new goods we were producing. His policies are delaying development because there isn't enough money to support the economy we have now. That's why the American dollar keeps going up in value," David said. "And he's certainly not going to want to issue enough money to support the economy of the USE as a whole. So there is likely to be a continuing shortage of money."

"If you people aren't issuing enough money, how are you running your business?"

"With Dutch guilders, Spanish doubloons, Holy Roman Empire *reichsthaler*. Which isn't doing good things to the economies of those places."

Herr Krause didn't look convinced. David understood that. Most people thought of money as having some sort of intrinsic value, especially in the seventeenth-century world of silver and, occasionally, gold coins. "Don't worry about it, Herr Krause. If you don't want American dollars, I'm happy enough to give you silver and let you pay a surcharge when you get the silver from me and another when you have to turn it back into American dollars to buy the stuff you want."

Krause slapped the table. "I don't want silver. I want steam engines, reapers, and water pumps. That's why I'm here in Magdeburg with a chest full of silver *reichsthaler*, which aren't buying me a cursed thing.

" 'There is a six month waiting list, Herr Krause.' 'There aren't any of those available, Herr Krause.' 'Check back in a few weeks. We are hoping for a new shipment then.' I have been—" Herr Krause threw up his hands, his frustration showing through his cynical persona."

"I was hoping that Herr Bartley of OPM could help me acquire some reapers, perhaps some seed. Maize would be very good. Instead, I have Lieutenant Bartley offering me silver, which won't buy me anything and assuring me that paper is even better. But, Lieutenant Bartley, paper American dollars won't buy me reapers, either. There are no reapers to be had, not for silver or paper."

David leaned back in his chair and smiled. "As it happens, I know the owners of USE Steel. I imagine something could be worked out."

∞ ∞ ∞

That meeting set the pattern. It wasn't universal, but David was increasingly finding people who were willing to pay a premium to "get it now." And that allowed him to get good deals for goods that the army would collect en route as it moved into Saxony. Goods to supplement what they were getting from the logistics train.

July 8, 1635
Higgins Hotel Dining Room

"How are you doing, Darlene?" Delia Higgins asked as Darlene tried to maneuver into a chair. It was getting close to her due date, and she was spending a lot of time shifting from one uncomfortable position to the next.

"Well, if the baby would quit playing kickball with my bladder, I would be a lot more comfortable," Darlene said. They were in the dining room of the Higgins Hotel, mostly because Darlene wasn't willing to just sit in her room. She had finally started her maternity leave because of how soon the baby was expected, but now she was going stir crazy. "It's all Johan's fault, and now he has run off to the army like a little kid running off to join the circus."

"Somehow, Johan doesn't strike me as the running-off sort."

"Maybe not. But I don't get how the down-timers react to us."

"How do you mean?" Delia asked.

Darlene hadn't known Delia Higgins up-time, hadn't met her until she had moved into the hotel with Johan, so Darlene wasn't sure just how to explain what she meant. Especially since David Bartley was Delia's grandson.

"Young Master David, Johan is a perfectly capable man. There is no reason in the world for him to follow your grandson around, cap in hand."

"Interesting you should put it that way," Delia said. "He arrived at our door, quite literally, cap in hand. And a pretty ragged cap it was too.

There are as many ways of responding to up-timers as there are down-timers. You get the ones like Gretchen Richter, who are more up-timer than the up-timers about the equality of all men. Then you get the ones who think of up-timers as a sort of curious peasant with a few special skills. But the way Johan acts toward us isn't that unusual. He grew up in a world where the classes were a lot more distinct and a lot more fixed than ours are. And there was no way our arrival was going to throw that training out the window. Instead, he fit us into it. We became the nobility—the way nobility was supposed to be. The funny thing is . . . well, at least the thing I hadn't thought about, was that it doesn't blind him to our faults, not at all. He is perfectly aware that he is a better bargainer than I am, or even than David is, though he's spent the last four years giving David an advanced course in bargaining."

"Fine. He likes you. I can accept that. And he is fond of David, sort of like David is his son or nephew or something. But why the deference?"

"Because that's what he's comfortable with," Delia said, with some asperity. "Don't think I didn't try to get him to stop. Well, I admit, I gave up pretty fast and never threatened to fire him or anything over it. He just is who he is, and I've learned to respect that." She gave Darlene a hard look. "If your marriage is going to work, you're going to have to learn to respect it too."

Darlene wasn't the least bit pleased with the lecture. "Does that mean he has to follow David off into the army when I'm nine months pregnant?"

"I think that's as much about the USE as it is about David," Delia said thoughtfully. "Not everyone who is dedicated to the new nation we are trying to build here is a firebrand. Johan spent most of his life as a soldier. He's doing his bit. Just like David is."

"You don't think he'd have gone if David hadn't?" Darlene asked.

"Maybe not. No, probably not. But that's not the same thing as him following David into the army. His deference to David—" Delia paused. "I think he uses David as sort of a moral check. As his guide into the morality of the twentieth century."

Chapter 11—Welcome Home, Daddy

July 9, 1635
Third Division Headquarters, Magdeburg

"You have a telegraph message, Sergeant," said the runner.

"From?" Johan asked. He received quite a few of them in the course of business.

"Grantville."

Johan took the folded sheet and signed the kid's book, then flipped it open.

BORN 12:37 AM, JULY 9, 1635 A BOY
8 LBS, 6 OZ, 22 IN. HANS DAVID KIPPER
AND YOU MISSED IT
DARLENE

"Is eight pounds big?" Johan wondered, as he tried to grapple with the idea that he was a father.

"Eight pounds of what?" David asked, his head still buried in a report.

"Baby!"

David's head came up. He looked at Johan and apparently found what he saw in Johan's face quite amusing. "I wouldn't ask Darlene that particular question," he said, laughing. "She may send you off to see Dr. Snipley."

Johan had seen horses gelded. And cattle and, well, whatever they said about minor surgery, the images and memories brought to mind by Dr. Susanna Shipley's nickname of Dr. Snipley didn't make him comfortable. "I'll keep quiet about it."

"I can spare you for a few days, and you can take a train to see her," David said. "You can catch up to us on the road. Or, the way things are going, you might get back before we leave." The logistics of moving a division and—even worse—an army even the relatively short distance into Saxony was not simple or easy. The delays had mounted as the up-time and down-time logistics tried to mesh. There was TacRail, as they had used in the Lübeck campaign, which they could use in Saxony, and there were the Elbe and Saale rivers, which would get them to well within striking distance, so the transport problems should be minor. But they weren't. For one thing, this army was better armed and equipped than any other army in the seventeenth century, as well as considerably better fed, all without raping the countryside as they went through.

"You might at that, sir," Johan said with a smile. He had a much more sanguine attitude toward the supply problems they were facing. By the standards he had used throughout his military career, they were going to war in luxury. Not the officers so much: mostly it was the enlisted men who were benefiting. They were marching to war in good army boots with wool socks and new uniforms, even underdrawers. It was no wonder this army had an unbelievable esprit de corps. And that spirit was, in Johan's view, worth the delay. John George of Saxony wasn't going anywhere, after all. Besides, it meant that he would be able to go home and see his son before he went into battle. "Yes, sir," Johan said. "I would like that."

"Well, good luck then, Johan." David grinned. "It looks like you will be going into danger before I do."

July 10, 1635
Higgins Hotel

"Welcome home, Herr Kipper," said the clerk at the front desk of the Higgins Hotel with a big grin. "And, congratulations."

Johan smiled and waved but didn't slow on his trip to the elevator. The elevator girl congratulated him as well while the car made its way up. Young Master David had released him immediately upon their receiving the telegraph message on the morning of the 9th, but there had been a very necessary talk with Beckmann before he could leave. Johan managed to catch the noon steamer out of Magdeburg, which got him to Haale by six in the evening, but the evening train to Grantville didn't leave till nine. And it was full, so he couldn't get a sleeping berth. He sat up on the bench as the train stopped at every little village between Haale and Grantville, and had gotten off it, exhausted, at seven in the morning of the tenth of July. The elevator jerked to a stop and the girl opened the door.

Johan opened the door to their suite on the floor just below the penthouse and heard a baby crying. He rushed in and saw the wet nurse—who Darlene insisted was a nanny—moving toward a crib, then another baby started crying in another room. The wet nurse had her own baby and had moved in shortly before Johan had left for Magdeburg.

Maria looked over at him and said, "You're late."

"I know. I was busy."

"Humph."

"Where is Darlene?"

Maria pointed with her chin, both hands being busy in one of the cribs, and Johan headed for the master bedroom.

"You're late," Darlene said. She was sitting in a rocking chair, with a small, wrinkled creature at her breast.

"Traffic," Johan said. "There's a lot of it between here and Magdeburg."

"How's the war going?"

"Never mind that. How are you?"

"Not so bad. Tired. The baby hasn't slept for more than a couple of hours at a stretch, but Maria has been a big help. We've talked about it and we'll take it in shifts, Maria taking care of both of them while I sleep and me taking care of both of them while she sleeps. Come see!"

And Johan went to see his son in Darlene's arms. "He's beautiful," Johan said. And he was, or at least he seemed so to Johan. Though he looked like any baby, somehow at the same time, he was Johan's, and infinitely unique.

∞ ∞ ∞

"I should have stayed in Magdeburg where it was safe," Johan muttered as he looked at the truly disgusting goop that was filling the cloth diaper of his son. It looked bad enough, but the smell! At least in the army he wouldn't be facing chemical weapons. Mike Stearns had insisted on that. Johan pulled a moist wipe from the heated "clean" pail and wiped the little fellow's bum. Then, wishing he had a pair of long tongs to handle it with, he picked up the diaper and put it in the covered "dirty" pail. They really should be hiring experts to handle this part. It wasn't like they couldn't afford it. Why Darlene insisted that he had to do this, he couldn't understand.

"I love you, kid, but I don't see why I have to prove it by wiping your bum. I can wait till you're old enough to talk and tell you stories and teach you to shoot or fish or something." Johan didn't say it very loudly, though. Darlene insisted he had to bond with Hans David by taking care of him this way, or he would be uncomfortable around him. Johan didn't buy it, but she had books to prove it—or said she did, anyway.

Johan harbored a secret suspicion that it was just her way of punishing him for getting her pregnant in the first place. Johan grinned and tickled Hans David's little belly, carefully avoiding the messy bits, then finished cleaning him off and moved him to the new diaper.

Chapter 12—Professionals Study Logistics

July 11, 1635
Colonel McAdam's Office

"The Third Division could make a profit on the deal, sir," David told Colonel McAdam. "We would be buying the stuff at golden corridor prices, then transporting it with the division, so no tolls or duties—no bandits for that matter—then selling at outland prices."

"Golden corridor?"

"Yes, sir. The Elbe up to the rail head and the rail line up to the Ring of Fire. The prices for most finished goods are lower in the corridor than just about anywhere else in the world. Still high by up-time standards, but . . . " David shrugged. For the most part, he didn't remember up-time that well any more, certainly not up-time prices. Prices for finished goods were low in the corridor and the price of labor was high, relative to the rest of the world. That wasn't constant, just an average. And people that didn't have the production machines tended to have real trouble competing. But that was another reason why the merchants and want-to-be manufacturers in places like Saxony were so desperate for nuts and bolts. "If the Third Division can bring pots and pans, nails and screws, and so forth with us, the local merchants will show up begging to sell us their grain so that they can buy our pots and pans."

But Colonel McAdam clearly wasn't impressed with David's notion. He gave one of those short sharp shakes of his head. "Pots and pans weigh a lot more than silver coins, and paper money weighs even less than silver. If they'll come for pots and pans, they'll come for silver."

The short, sharp, head shake had told David that the colonel had made up his mind. So he didn't point out that they would be "buying" the silver for precisely the same price they would be "selling" it for, but the pots and pans would sell for considerably more in Saxony than they would cost in the corridor.

Colonel McAdam wouldn't sign off on the division buying trade goods to cart with them on campaign.

"In that case, Colonel, may I have your permission to do it on my own?"

"What do you mean?"

"I buy the goods, I hire the drovers."

"You have that kind of money, Lieutenant?"

"Yes, sir."

Colonel McAdam leaned back, causing the wood and canvas chair to creak ominously. He scratched his jaw, and for a moment David thought he might be reconsidering. Instead he sat back up and said, "Fine. You do it, but you're going to pay a fee to Third Division for every ton mile."

They bargained for a while and David had to threaten to drop the notion twice before he got a rate he could live with. But he got a signed agreement to the effect that his drovers could travel with the army and a set price for anything he sold to the army.

July 12, 1635
Third Army Headquarters, Magdeburg

"I need some drovers, Sergeant Beckmann," David said. He was as angry as he could remember being. Colonel McAdam's casual dismissal of his idea to carry low-volume manufactured goods to trade for supplies had pissed him off, probably a great deal more than it should have. And he had been thinking about it for the last two days.

"Yes, sir. What for?"

"We are going to have a trading mission go along with the army when we go to Saxony."

Beckmann hesitated, then said, "Sir, I thought the colonel didn't like that idea."

"He didn't, but I got him to agree that I could do it. I think he figured I would be doing it on a small scale. But he didn't say that."

"Just what sort of scale are you figuring on, sir?"

"Just as large as we can manage. Look, Saxony has had trouble getting so much as a cigarette lighter since John George's treason. Not because there has been any sort of effective blockade, but just because no one was making any special effort to get them manufactured goods and there were other people that wanted them closer."

"Not to mention the fact that there doesn't appear to be any silver in Saxony anymore. Just John George's paper, and it's best used to wipe your ass with."

"Right. But the farmers have gone on growing their crops and the carders have kept on carding and spinsters kept on spinning. At least some. So there are a lot of goods with no place to trade them. And the army is going to need them, at least the food and probably some of the cloth."

Beckmann looked doubtful and David knew why. Saxony was probably not as productive as David was describing. Aside from everything else, John George's policies had made the hope of profit as fanciful as hoping a genie granted your wishes when you rubbed a lamp. So the folks in Saxony were probably working no harder than they had to. David didn't care. If they were going to get the supplies that the army needed, they were going to have to trade for them, and David intended to have trade goods to do it with.

"Ah, sir . . . who's going to pay for the goods? And for that matter, the wagons and the horses and the drovers?"

"I am."

July 25, 1635
Kipper Suite, Higgins Hotel

"What are we having for dinner?" Johan asked Darlene, holding up a menu.

"I don't know about you, but I'm having a porterhouse steak, a baked potato, and broccoli in hollandaise sauce. Medium rare on the steak, sour cream and butter on the potato. And bread. Don't forget the bread. Cheesecake for dessert."

Johan looked at her with something like awe. She had been eating like that while she was pregnant and Johan had sort of expected it to stop once the baby was born, but it turned out that she used up almost as much food making milk to feed the baby as she did making the baby. So Darlene was eating like a bodybuilder and losing weight. Which all came as a great surprise to Johan, but he was told that it was pretty standard.

Johan had some of Darlene's famous lamb fried orzo, which recipe the Higgins Hotel chef had somehow gotten hold of. Johan knew nothing about how the chef had gotten it, though Darlene shot him suspicious looks every time he ordered it.

Johan ordered it anyway. It was good.

"Any word from David?" Darlene asked. Johan had been back for just over two weeks, spending most of his time with Darlene. But part of his time was spent with the merchants of Grantville, making sure that the various businesses and enterprises didn't suffer too much from David's being off in the army. To be honest, they mostly weren't suffering at all. David Bartley tended to succeed himself right out of a job. He set up enterprises that were quite capable of running without him, and they did.

"Yes. They seem to have gotten most of the kinks out of the supply lines, and David wants to take industrial goods with the army to trade for supplies they might need on the march."

"Why?"

"Because the people that we are going to be dealing with in Saxony aren't very trusting of paper money, even American dollars, and they aren't even all that trusting of silver."

"So David wants to send trade goods with the army. That almost makes sense."

"A lot of the stuff Master David thinks of are that way. They do make sense, but they are so out of the ordinary way of thinking that they don't seem to."

"Well, that's not how I would put it, but he does seem to be successful. So the army is going to march into Saxony with sewing machines on their backs?"

"Not the army. Master David suggested it to Colonel McAdam, but the colonel wasn't exactly thrilled with the idea. He figures that if they are going to take stuff into Saxony to spend for supplies they should take silver. It's a lot easier to carry than sewing machines or typewriters."

"If not the army, then who?"

"David is going to ship them himself, hiring drovers and wagons to go with the army and carry the goods."

"Isn't that pretty risky?"

"Not unless the army of Gustav Adolph gets defeated by the army of John George of Saxony." Johan snorted.

"Okay, but I mean what if the enemy gets behind the army and attacks the wagon train?"

"Not very likely," Johan said.

∞ ∞ ∞

"Wheels?" Darlene asked the next day.

"Wheel hubs," Johan confirmed, "and heavy gauge steel wire."

"What on earth for?"

"Transportation mostly. The hubs are machined in a factory so are very consistent quality, and the wires that connect them to the rims are adjustable . . ."

"Bicycle wheels?"

Johan paused and thought. "Yes, sort of. More like motorcycle wheels, I think. Heavier, and they will probably end up with wooden rims."

"What are they going to do with a bunch of wooden-rimmed motorcycle wheels in Saxony?"

"Put them on wagons. I would think also on wheelbarrows and handcarts. It's just one more of the ways that up-time knowledge is mixing with down-time necessity to make new products. They use them all over the place in the State of Thuringia-Franconia and Magdeburg Province, but they haven't gotten to Saxony yet."

"So why are you buying them rather than David? The factory's in Kamburg. It's closer to David than to you, isn't it?"

"Not really, but that's not the point. The business manager for the factory is located about four floors below us, and I can make the deal without leaving the hotel. For that matter, I could make the deal over the phone without leaving our bed. Just pick up the phone." Johan leered at her.

"Forget it, buster. Even if I was ready for that, you talking wheel rims on the phone is not exactly a turn on."

Johan sighed histrionically. "In that case, I will get in the elevator, go down and talk to the man in person."

"Put on some clothes first." Darlene snorted and continued to get ready for her day. She was still struggling between being worn out by the pregnancy and being increasingly bored with nothing to do. Well, not nothing. Little Hans David was plenty of work, as was Maria's little girl, but they divided up the work and were managing quite well. Besides, the diapers were cleaned by the diaper service, and the apartment by the hotel staff, which made life much easier and her recovery from the pregnancy quicker.

August 1, 1635
Grantville Train Station

Johan kissed Darlene on the train platform, feeling both embarrassed and a little like a hero in one of those old up-time movies. He wasn't sure which one. He had seen a lot of them. But with the train station and the uniform, little Hans David and especially Darlene, it felt like that.

Then he climbed aboard the train and headed back to Magdeburg. The army and Third Division had started its march toward Saxony. Johan would meet it in route.

August 4, 1635
En route to Saxony

Johan rode along in the trail of the army. Wagons and push carts piled with goods, as well as ammunition and other military stores, stretched out for miles behind the advancing army. And as he rode, he wondered how Master David had managed to buy so much. David Bartley was wealthy by any standards, but not nearly as rich as most people thought.

While he was at OPM he had controlled incredible wealth, but as the name stated, that was other people's money for the most part.

This was a lot of goods, and Johan began to worry. David's credit was good, incredibly good, especially for a man as young as he was. But he had to have stretched it to the limit, and if this didn't work David could be in a lot of trouble. Suddenly Johan realized why he hadn't been invited into this project. David wasn't nearly as sure of the results as he was pretending to be and David being David, he hadn't wanted anyone else's money in something this risky.

Johan began to worry as he hadn't worried when he was in Grantville with Darlene. He shouldn't have left David alone. There was more than just shell and shot that could cause damage in war. Especially this sort of war.

Johan spurred his horse. He needed to get forward as quickly as he could. Not that he had a clue what he'd do when he got there.

August 5, 1635
Third Army Headquarters, Camp En route to Saxony

"Beckmann, why the hell didn't you call me?" Johan scowled at the sergeant.

"About what?"

"About all these trade goods , curse it !"

"I know it's a lot, but he must have the money. He's the one who told me to organize it."

"Not this much! Not without borrowing against almost everything he has."

"But why?" Beckmann asked. "I know he was pissed at Colonel McAdam about not having the division do it, but . . . " Beckmann paused then continued, sounding resentful. "You think it's going to be that profitable?"

"No, you idiot. I think it's that risky. And so does Master David, else he'd have put us both in it. If he is doing this much on his own, it's because he thinks it needs doing and is afraid that it won't work."

It was no use. Beckmann was looking at him like he was nuts. The sergeant didn't understand why Johan wouldn't just be relieved to be out of a risky venture when there were so many that were safer and just as profitable.

"Never mind," Johan said. "The money's on the table. It's too late to do anything but play the hand."

Beckmann nodded and Johan could read in the sergeant's face that he was just glad it wasn't his money, while Johan was wishing that at least some of it was his.

August, 1635
Saxon Plain, near Zwenkau

David, Johan, Sergeant Beckmann, and the rest of their merry band of supply clerks saw the battle of Zwenkau from a safe distance. They were guarding the supply train, which included David's train as well as the more military supplies. They were close enough to see the battle but, barring a stray bullet, in no danger. And David, who was not of high enough rank to have been briefed on the plan, started the day by wondering if Mike Stearns had gone off his rocker or if he was just an idiot glory hound who was going to get a lot of people killed—hopefully including himself so he couldn't do it again. The Third Division was advancing on its own, leaving a gap for the enemy to take advantage of. There were lots of battles throughout history that had been lost by just such idiocy, and David began to wonder what the Saxons would do with his wagon train after they had trashed the USE Army.

David looked over at Johan. "Well, aren't you glad now that I didn't let you invest in this?" he asked disgustedly. "At least Darlene will be a rich widow."

"Don't jump too soon, young master," Johan said. "I don't know the Prince personally, but I don't think he's the sort to go galloping off after glory. It doesn't fit the man."

"No, it doesn't," David said thoughtfully. "What do you think is going on, Johan?"

"I'm not sure. But if it's not a fool's errand, it almost has to be the setting of a trap for those fellows over there." He pointed at the Saxon army. "And if it's a trap, I don't think they will be thrilled when it closes on them."

David nodded, willing enough to be instructed by a man who had been in almost as many battles as he had read about. "Still, whether the trap works or not, it's likely to be hard on the bait."

"Maybe. Depends on how tough the bait is, sometimes."

∞ ∞ ∞

"Set up over there," David said. The army was still cleaning up after the battle of Zwenkau, but the merchants were already arriving. News of the length and quality of the army's supply train had traveled ahead—helped, no doubt, by the fact that David had mentioned it to every Saxon merchant he had talked to in the last month. Now that the battle was over, the merchants were rushing in with wagons filled with grain and other wagons filled with wool and woad and anything else that the land could be encouraged to produce.

The wagon full of wagon wheel hubs moved off in the direction David had indicated and was followed by one filled with rulers and typewriters, hole punchers and punched cards. Also card sorters.

"We'll only be here for a day or so," David heard Beckmann tell a merchant. "Then we follow the army toward Dresden."

∞ ∞ ∞

They were in Dresden for over a week. Well, outside of Dresden anyway. The wounded were billeted in Dresden, but the rest of the army wasn't. They sold manufactured goods in Dresden and bought the excess produce of Saxony . . . and perhaps more than the excess.

∞ ∞ ∞

"Beckmann, you idiot," Johan said coldly. "I ought to let them hang you. Hell, man, I ought to pull the lever."

"But Lieutenant Bartley left us out of it! I was just trying to make a little on the side."

"Master David paid for the goods he sold. He didn't take them from the army."

Beckmann had no answer for that, but he still looked a bit resentful. Beckmann was a skilled criminal and a persuasive con man, but he needed considerable watching or he wandered into trouble. He was just as good at persuading himself that the ice was warm and the sun cold as he was at persuading anyone else.

"It's not like we're short of tents," Beckmann said. Which was true. The army had been sent over a thousand extra tents and most of them had gone to Third Division. The tents were made of hemp-based sailcloth and were double-walled squad tents. Put together, they were a fairly decent house. Johan didn't know how the army had gotten so many, but the tent maker was a crony of Prime Minister Wettin.

"What did they want with squad tents?" Johan asked, curiosity getting the better of him.

"I haven't got a clue, but I think it was the heavy panels of fabric they were after," Beckmann said. "Look, we were just carrying them around with us and we never would have used them. And I got forty-two oxen for them, which I sold to the army for stores."

Johan shook his head. Beckmann was about to be broke and a corporal. Again.

It was starting to look like a tradition.

The situation was all complicated by the fact that Master David had made a fortune by selling the trade goods that he'd bought in Magdeburg to Third Division for American dollars at a huge profit after the merchants of Saxony sold everything they could scrape together.

It was all perfectly legal, and considering that David had documentary evidence that he had first tried to get Third Division involved, it wasn't even iffy. But that didn't keep the rumors from spreading, and David didn't want to be known as a war profiteer.

September, 1635
Kipper Suite, Higgins Hotel

"They're going to Poland," Darlene said, with more bitterness than she'd intended.

"We're in a war, Darlene," Delia Higgins said. "And it's close, not like Vietnam or Korea or even World War II. It's not across an ocean. It's right next door. And if our men don't go, our enemies will come right to our doorsteps."

"Though I think Gustav is as stupid as Johnson was," Connie, Darlene's mother, interjected. "We should have stayed out of Poland, just like we should have stayed out of Vietnam. Let's just hope we don't have a damn McNamara this time."

"Which is beside the point, if anything ever was," Delia said. "Not that I disagree about Poland. But the point is, we don't just need young men like David. We need old vets like Johan to take care of them."

"Neither David or Johan needs to go, dammit!" Darlene insisted, feeling unreasonable even as she said it. "They contribute to the war effort just fine on the homefront. Isn't that what starting up your sewing machine company was all about?"

"Yes. But David was fourteen at the time and you may not know it, Darlene, but Trent and Brent's older brother was in the Battle of the Crapper. So was Jeff, as you might have heard."

"So was your brother," Darlene's mother said.

"I know, but at least now Allen is safe in the reserves." Darlene knew she was whining and she knew she was wrong, but the babies, both of them, had colic at the moment, and if Hans David was loud, little Maria Josephine had a voice like an air raid siren. And, well, it had been over six weeks since the baby and, well, she missed Johan. She had assumed that he would at least get to come home and visit. After the quick work they had made of Saxony, she had hoped all this military nonsense would be done with.

Connie looked at Darlene and said, "I don't care if you're horny. You need to get over this whining. It's not like you're the one who is in the sights of the men with cannon. This is what women have always done, Darlene. We did it in the Revolution, the Civil War, and all the other wars. We hold it together so that there's something for our men to come back to."

September, 1635
Dresden

"How are we going to get all this crap to Poland?" Colonel McAdam asked. David had sold plenty of the goods they had brought and Third Division had bought a lot more grain, cloth, and leather than it actually needed. But there were still drop forges, typewriters, and other such things for selling, and Third Division had way too much grain and cloth.

David looked at the massive piles of cloth and the stack of grain sacks. "We aren't. We are going to leave it here in the care of the CoC, who will sell it, take a commission, and send the money back to Magdeburg. I'll have my agents buy more in Magdeburg and send it from there, probably down the Elbe and along the Baltic coast." All of which would be a lot easier if they were going to be there to watch over it, but Third Division was marching overland to Poland. The Third Division was to be the southern wing of the invading army.

"I don't know, Lieutenant Bartley." Colonel McAdam rubbed his right temple, then scratched his chin. "When the goods followed us, they were protected by the army. Sending them by the Baltic route will be risky."

"Who is going to attack Third Division goods or even inspect them? We are Gustav's army and Mike Stearns' division."

"I don't know. I think we should arrange to have the goods shipped overland to join us in route."

"The roads suck, sir." David said, knowing full well what McAdam was actually concerned about. David had paid Third Division a fee for every mile where his goods were protected by the division. Overland meant that David would be paying that fee all the way to Poland. The sea route meant he wouldn't. "It would take them forever to catch up with the army, and the risk as they went overland through what amounts to a war zone would be just as great. I prefer the sea route."

"Well, I think the supply corps should receive a bigger share for the risk."

"If you feel the risk is too great, you don't need to invest, sir."

"I could deny you permission."

"Considering how important the goods were to the army—not just Third Division, but the whole army—in the Saxony campaign, I would have to bring your refusal of permission to the general's attention." David was bluffing. But by now, under the tutelage of Johan Kipper, Karl

Schmidt, and Herr Kunze, David was pretty good at bluffing. Colonel McAdam backed down.

Which was a really good thing because David wasn't at all sure that Mike Stearns would approve of what he had done, much less support him.

"We can't use Beckmann, so you're going to have to oversee things in Magdeburg and Grantville," David told Johan Kipper two hours later. "I'm going to be with the army and someone who is familiar with the process is going to have to shepherd it through the merchants at Magdeburg. See if you can worm a couple more steam engines out of Adolph and talk to Franz about some canned fruit." Canned fruit was a delicacy in this world, available but expensive, and in winter worth its weight in gold. Well, silver.

"And talk to Stephen Kruger about freeze-dried meats. Yes, I know, David. But are you sure you can manage without me?"

David smiled at the older man, in many ways more his father than his father had ever been. "I'll be fine, Johan. I'll be fine."

"Once you get things organized, stay with the first load of goods and join us wherever we end up."

September, 1635
River boat, en route to Magdeburg

The army was marching east, and Johan Kipper was on a river boat heading north to Magdeburg. It wasn't what he would have preferred. Given his druthers, he and David would be in Grantville. He would be playing with the baby and loving Darlene, and David would be setting up businesses and chasing pretty girls as a young man ought.

Johan looked over the railing at the muddy water, feeling almost as muddy and brown as the water looked. Then he shook himself and got back to work. There was paperwork to do; there always was. And it was best to keep busy.

September, 1635
Magdeburg Docks

Johan moved toward the ramp with his mind on the business of the day, not paying much attention to what was going on around him.

"Johan!"

Johan's head popped up like a jack in the box at Darlene's voice. There on the docks was his wife, with little Hans David in her arms. And Maria, along with her own baby, was right behind her.

Johan rushed forward all of two steps before he was blocked by the other passengers. He just had to wait. It was, he thought, smiling broadly, horrible how real life got in the way of romantic moments. He waited his turn, then held his wife and chucked little Hans under the chin. "What are you doing here?"

"I took some time off. Grete is handling the Twinlo Palace and it only took a few days to fix the pressure gauge connections for the new steam power plant."

The steam power plant was the main power system that Twinlo was working on. It was intended to be a stand-alone system that could be mass produced. There were already electrical power plants in operation that used steam, internal combustion, water or wind to turn the generators, but they were one-off jobs and as expensive as one-off jobs always are. Brent's goal was a mass-produced power system that could be produced cheaply, relatively speaking. That was one of the reasons that the twins recruited Darlene.

"Fine, but . . ."

"I wanted to see you and I looked at our bank book. That was a bit of a shock. I knew you were rich, but seeing it . . . Well, I decided I was going to spend a little of it. Come down here, see the opera and just, by the way, my husband."

Johan was smiling like to crack his face, but he couldn't stop.

For the next several days Darlene shopped and saw the sights in Magdeburg while Johan arranged for the transport of goods to the Third Division. And they talked about the world and the war and why they had to go.

"Gustav is right, Darlene. The Polish Vasas are a constant thorn in his side and the way they treat their peasants is a crime, or at least it should be."

Darlene wasn't convinced. It wasn't so much that she disagreed with anything Johan had said, but she didn't see why it was the USE's problem. The force the Poles had sent to support John George of Saxony and George William of Brandenburg was no more than a token. Just rude, not a real cause to go to war.

They agreed to disagree and to enjoy Magdeburg together.

It was over much too soon. Johan followed a load of goods onto a river boat and was off to Poland.

Chapter 13—The Exchange Corps

October, 1635
Zielona Góra

David came out of Mike Stearns' office, shaking his head and mumbling. "The barges aren't carrying enough for this. Not nearly enough." He marched across the camp, still muttering and thinking, to the stockade. The stockade was a tent next to the supply depot, where again-Corporal Beckmann resided.

"Hello, Toby," David said to the guard. Toby was a mercenary who preferred Toby to Tobias, and he had the guard detail to watch after Beckmann and the other members of Third Division who had been drunk on duty, mouthed off to their officers, or otherwise incurred the minor displeasure of the powers that be. "I have orders to get Beckmann out of hock."

Toby laughed. "That's fine. My guests are being little lambs, Lieutenant Bartley."

About now all of Toby's "guests" were absolutely thrilled that they were in tents under guard rather than in the mass grave with the perpetrators of the massacre at Świebodzin. Until two days ago, the other divisions had felt that General Stearns was a soft and gentle man. They didn't anymore. Volley guns at point blank range didn't leave much and what they had left had been dumped in a hole and covered over. Stearns had also executed officers over the atrocity and the Third Division was in shock over the whole thing.

David showed Toby the orders, and Toby yelled for Beckmann.

Third Division Supply Depot

Colonel McAdam looked up as David came in, followed by Beckmann. "Generals are silly things, Lieutenant. Much too busy with affairs of state and the like to know how to deal with the Beckmanns of this world. Was that all the general wanted?"

"I'm supposed to form the Exchange Corps," David said. He didn't bother to mention his promotion to captain.

"What's that?"

David started to smile.

"Apparently, whatever I want it to be. It's supposed to keep the Third Division in beans and underwear, but other than that, he pretty much left it up to me." David was grinning.

He turned to Beckmann. "See if you can find a set of captain's bars for me. And, Sergeant, dig up some sergeant's stripes for yourself." Then David remembered a line from an old movie. "And maybe you should get them with zippers this time, considering how often you're taking them off and putting them on."

"You mean it's whatever we want it to be," Colonel McAdam interrupted. "A colonel still outranks a captain, and I'm still the head of Third Division supplies."

"Not quite, sir. The Exchange Corps is to be a separate unit, responsible directly to the general. However, we will need to coordinate with S4."

∞ ∞ ∞

"Coordinate what, Captain?" McAdam said cautiously. He was by now fully aware that pissing matches with Lieutenant Bartley had not tended to go his way. He *suspected* that pissing matches with Captain Bartley, commander of the Exchange Corps, were going to be absolute disasters. Not that he liked the arrogant bastard, but he figured discretion was indicated.

"Honestly, sir, I don't know yet. What I am sure of is that I am going to need to use Third Division's radios rather a lot over the next few days. I have access to Third Division's discretionary funds, but I don't think they are going to be nearly enough. I'm going to need money."

McAdam leaned back in his chair and considered. Third Division could have gotten a share of the tremendous profits that Bartley gained when he shipped goods in the army's trail into Saxony. For that matter, McAdam could have. "Will you be needing investors, Captain?"

"Almost certainly. I'll be able to get some from Franz Kunze, the Stone family, and, of course, from Karl Schmidt, but yes, Colonel, I think I'm going to need to raise more than they are likely to have on hand."

"In that case, Captain, count me in."

McAdam almost laughed at the captain's expression then.

October 1, 1635
Boar's Head Inn, near Zielona Góra

"Would you be interested in investing in the Third Division Exchange Corps, Major Barclay?"

"That depends. What *is* the Third Division Exchange Corps, Captain Bartley?"

Three David Bs sat in the small inn. Two captains and a major.

The third David was Captain David Blodger, the up-timer quartermaster for technical supplies. They had gotten together in part because their names were similar enough that their mail and other records sometimes got confused, and because David Blodger was interested in the work being done at Twinlo Park and Major Barclay was interested in up-timer finance methods. It was Captain David Blodger who asked, "Is this like Other People's Money?"

"Sort of." David Bartley snorted, but didn't comment on the fact that he hadn't known about OPM till it was basically a done deal. "General Stearns wants me to come up with a way to supply Third Division without any supply train."

"I thought you were already doing that," Major Barclay said. "I saw those boats your man brought upriver. There was a fortune in them."

David Bartley shook his head. "Not even close, sir. What I've done is managed to fill in the missing bits. The standard S4 procedures have provided most of the goods. I'm not sure, but I think that General Stearns is afraid that the Poles might cut our supply lines at some point."

"Maybe, but I doubt it," Major Barclay said. "Cutting a supply line is easier said than done."

"So how are you going to produce this miracle?" Captain David Blodger asked.

"I've been thinking about that," David Bartley said, "and it's going to take more money than I can raise personally. The stuff Johan brought up is a drop in the bucket."

"I will want to look over the contracts and see the . . . what is it you call it . . . the prospectus? I will want to look at that," David Barclay said.

"We don't have anything like that yet, I'm afraid," David said. "This has all come up rather suddenly."

"Well, when you get it, I want to see it. But in the meantime, what are you planning?"

"For one thing a permanent store here in Zielona Góra. We are going to have to establish a permanent presence so that customers won't be worried about us running off, leaving their orders unfilled."

"So a building here and more for every city and village that Third Division stops at?"

"Not every village but, yes, every major town." David Bartley smiled. David Barclay smiled back and waved his cup, calling for a refill of the white wine he was drinking.

David Bartley continued as the serving girl filled Barclay's cup. "And we are going to have to have contracts with, well . . ." Major Barclay started to take a drink as David continued. ". . . for instance, we are going to have to have a contract with Schmidt Steam to build us a thousand steam engines over the next year."

Wine flew across the table and Major David Barclay choked. "A . . . *cough . . . thousand* steam engines?"

David looked at the major in surprise. "Yes, of course. If Adolph is going to buy the extra machines and put on the extra crew that he will need to turn out the steam engines we need, he must be assured of a market. It would be best if we paid him in advance."

"Ah," said David Blodger with a grin. "That's our little David Bartley. Always thinking small." He, after all, hadn't had a mouth full of wine when he heard David's pronouncement.

"You don't think you will have difficulty selling a thousand steam engines in addition to the ones that Herr Schmidt is already building and with, of course, every blacksmith in Germany building their own?" Major Barclay asked.

"In Germany?" David shook his head. "If we had ten thousand to sell, they would disappear into Germany like rain in the desert."

"So why not order ten thousand?" Blodger asked.

"Because I don't have the money, not for that and the plows, typewriters, sewing machines, ready-to-wear clothing, nails, nuts, bolts, and all the other goods that Germany and Europe are crying out for."

"Even with us investing?"

"Even then," David said. "If I ordered ten thousand, Adolph would charge me five times the price per unit that he will charge for one thousand."

"What? Isn't that backwards?" Major Barclay asked and Captain Blodger nodded in agreement.

"Normally it would be," David Bartley agreed. "But one thousand extra in a year is pushing Adolph's capability. To get to ten thousand, he would have to hit up Ollie Reardon or David Marcantonio to produce even bigger machines. He would have to buy more steel—a lot more steel—enough to drive the price up even higher than it already is. As it is, we aren't going to get much of a discount for the large order, if we get any, and we might end up paying a premium." David Bartley shook his head. The economy of central Europe was gearing up as fast as it could, and the Third Division stores were going to push it even harder. It could only go so fast, no matter how much money you pushed at it.

October, 1635
Zielona Góra

Johan Kipper walked down the gangplank onto the docks of ruined Zielona Góra. Zielona Góra was part of Germany, or it should have been. It *had been* till George William had given it to the king of Poland in exchange for his aid, and as Johan looked around at the burned out buildings, he guessed it was again. But it had certainly put up one heck of a fight.

He was in charge of two steam-powered river boats that had steamed up the Oder River to the Odra River to here with surprisingly little trouble, considering they were going through a war zone. They were well armed, though, and the steaming upriver was still weird enough to scare off the superstitious. Not that they made particularly good time. Johan had managed to get just two eight-horsepower steam engines, one for each barge, and sometimes they barely made two knots against the current. But they didn't need teams on shore to pull them.

It had been hard work and anything but exciting, which was just fine with Johan. What wasn't fine with him was David in a battle without him.

He saw Master David walking up the pier, followed by Beckmann. He noted the new rank insignia on Captain Bartley's shoulders, and wondered what idiocy-called-gallantry the lad had been about to earn them.

Master David apparently saw something in Johan's expression, because he said, "It was fine, Johan, at least for me. I think the Hangman Regiment got hung out to dry, though."

"The Hangman Regiment?" Johan asked. He was familiar with the regiments of the division, and there wasn't a Hangman Regiment. At least, there hadn't been.

That was when David told him about Świebodzin.

"I wouldn't have thought that the Prince would do that," Johan said, not at all sure how he felt about it. It wasn't the sort of thing that you wanted a general doing to his own men.

"They earned it, Johan," Master David said, and his voice was again that of a lord. This time a lord pronouncing sentence.

Smiling now, Johan thought, *And people think up-timers are soft.* "So tell me about the battle. You said the Hangman got hung out to dry?"

David described the battle.

Johan nodded. "I wonder what Colonel Higgins did to piss off the Prince of Germany so soon after his promotion."

"I don't know. But whatever it was, the general apparently got over his mad. He went to see Jeff in the hospital."

"Well, it could be that he just needed them there, I guess," Johan agreed. "What are the troops saying about it?"

"It depends. A lot of them were pretty pissed at Jeff's guys after the general had them hang those rapist bastards. There was talk about the Hangman Regiment being General Stearns' bully boys, not real soldiers. And I've heard 'it couldn't have happened to a more deserving regiment' on more than one occasion. I know one thing, though. No one is wondering whether Jeff and his guys can take it anymore."

Johan nodded again and thought that might be the why right there, though it would take a pretty cold-blooded bastard to do that. *Let them get chewed on just to prove that they could take it.* That's hard. Johan shook himself. "How is the supply situation?"

"Not as good as it was in Saxony. We are farther from home and we have had less opportunity to prepare. And General Sterns is afraid it's going to get worse. That's why I'm a captain now, not because of some kind of derring-do. I've been put in charge of the Exchange Corps."

"What's the Exchange Corps?"

"I've been working on that ever since the general gave me the job. What we are going to have to do is become a retailer. A big retailer, along the lines of Walmart."

"Walmart?" Johan asked. "You've mentioned them before, but I don't think I ever got the details."

"Sarah did a paper on them while we were in Amsterdam," David explained. "On them and Sears and the other retailer chains. There were these really big companies back up-time that owned hundreds of stores all over the place. They bought in bulk and shipped goods everywhere. You could get anything from them. Just go to the local store and if they didn't have it, they could get it. What we need is the stores wherever Third Division happens to be. We have the one in Dresden where we left our leftovers after the Third Division took Saxony, and we have the one here."

Johan didn't comment on Master David's exaggeration of Third Division's role in the conquest of Saxony. It wasn't all that big an overstatement, and it was good for a young officer to have pride in his unit. It was even good for old sergeants. "That gives us two stores."

"We're going to have one in Magdeburg too." David said. "We don't really need the one there or the one we're going to set up in Badenburg. Those will just be for the profit. What we actually need is the name. We need the Third Division Commissary. No . . . I like that, but we need something that will resonate with the locals and not sound military. Third Division Superstore . . . um . . . *Supermarkt*."

"Why?" Johan asked.

"Because without a proper logistics train, we are going to need a logistics magnet. We are going to need the people to collect up their rye and sauerkraut, pigs and sheep, and bring them to us, because the Third Division Superstore is where they can sell their stuff and buy manufactured goods that in the normal course of events would never reach them at anything like a price they could pay."

"That's going to be expensive, Master David."

"Yes, I know. I'm going to hit up Franz Kunze and Karl Schmidt. Probably the Stones too. I've also been having conversations with the officers of Third Division, offering to let them invest. I've explained the risks, but I'm not sure how much they get it after the profits we made in Saxony. And now that we have your barges, the profit we are likely to make here." David shrugged. "Or maybe they do get it and just realize it's better to lose your shirt in a business venture than to lose your life because you didn't have the powder and shot to survive the battle."

Third Division Supply Depot

Johan started having his own conversations. He talked to the sergeants and the corporals throughout the division. He talked to the CoC organizers and discussed the investments in terms they would understand. "We're using Master David's connections to buy in the Golden Corridor where it's cheap, then using the army's tax-free status to ship it to the stores and selling the stuff out here where it's worth its weight in gold. We're going to make a fortune, and we're letting you fellows buy in cheap because you're part of the Prince's own, just like Master Bartley."

"I know he's rich, but the way I hear it, Bartley squeezes a buck till it's venison jerky," the sergeant said.

"He's not a man you want to try and cheat," Johan said. "But he is generous in his way. And he don't take advantage of them that don't have much."

October, 1635
Zielona Góra

After his talk with Colonel McAdams, David Bartley was busy. Not so busy that he failed to notice that the better part of Third Division was going off to war and he was in the rear area again. He knew the nature of his job meant that was often going to be the case, and a part of him was actually a little relieved. But that only made him resent it even more.

Even so, there was the rebuilding of Zielona Góra to see to and the acquisition of property on which to put the store, and Third Division had left them a radio. A radio that David could make good use of, in fact. A message reading:

NEED SEWING MACHINES AND OTHER GOODS SHIPPED TO ZIELONA GORA SOONEST. WHEN WILL THE CONTRACTS BE READY AND HOW MUCH FUNDING CAN YOU GET ME?

Was sent to Herr Franz Kunze, who was acting as David's primary agent in the Grantville area. Herr Kunze lived in Badenburg, but these days he kept an office in the Higgins Hotel for handling business. In Grantville he had phones and computers and printers so that contracts could be printed, signed, and notarized, all within hours.

Herr Kunze handed the telegraph to his son. "So, how much funding can we get him?"

"Quite a bit, but not enough for this, I don't think. Look, Papa, I like David. He's a good kid and pretty clever, but don't you think he's bitten off more than he can chew on this one?"

"No. Son, you're missing the point. It's not David Bartley who matters this time. It's Mike Stearns, the Prince of Germany."

"General Stearns didn't come up with this, Papa."

"No, of course not. But he authorized it. I don't know what's going to happen now that Gustav has been injured, but Stearns is the head of one of the most powerful factions in Germany. He could end up as the true prince of Germany."

Franz's son was looking at him doubtfully, so Franz continued. "I know it's not likely and you know it's not likely, but how many people know Mike Stearns? How many people will think about him and assume that if offered the crown, he would turn it down?"

Now his son nodded, and Franz shrugged. "Would you want to piss off the man that might be the next emperor of the United States of Europe? Or would you rather be invested in his own division's Exchange Corps?"

"All right. I can see how that would help, but I'm still not sure it will be enough to get the sort of money David wants from investors. Truthfully, Papa, this all makes me a bit nervous, the whole house of cards this economic boom is built on. Stocks and bonds and loans and build more and make faster and ship . . . Who can afford all the stuff we are making?"

"I know, and it makes me nervous too but we are well and truly on the tiger's back and getting off hasn't been an option for these last two years."

November, 1635
Zielona Góra

"We're going where?" Johan asked.

"Back to Saxony," the radio tech said. "I just got the word. Oxenstierna has ordered Third Division to support King Albrecht against a possible encroachment by the Hapsburgs—as if he hadn't already kicked their ass up to their shoulder blades."

"He's putting the Prince out of the way," Johan said, angrily. "Are we going?" Johan was ready to go after Oxenstierna himself.

"The Prince's orders," the tech said. "We are soldiers of the USE, not a private army."

"But Oxenstierna isn't even in our chain of command. He's Swedish. If he wants Albrecht reinforced, let him send a Swedish division. He has no right to be ordering units of the USE Army around."

"No, he doesn't. But Wettin does. He's the Prime Minister, duly elected."

"I don't like it."

"Truth to tell, Johan, I'm not all that thrilled with it, either. But thems the orders."

Chapter 14—Moving and Shaking

November, 1635

Grantville

*A*s it happened, Johan didn't march with the army to Saxony again. He was sent to Magdeburg, and this time on to Grantville, to oversee the organization of Third Division Exchange Corps Corporation.

"Hey," Darlene said, "I thought you were off in the army. What are you doing back here so soon? I have my lovers hiding in the closet and under the bed." She grinned wickedly.

"Never trust a soldier, girl. We show up at the most inconvenient times." Johan grinned back. "Come on out, fellows. The husband's home." He ostentatiously looked around. "Timid sorts, your lovers. I must say I'm disappointed in your taste if you've chosen such cowards as paramores."

"Oh, come here, you." She grabbed him and pulled him down for a kiss. "But, seriously, what brought you back? This Exchange Corps everyone is talking about?"

"Yes. Partly it is organizational stuff, but mostly I'm here to beg as much production as I can get to go to the stores we want to set up."

November, 1635
Higgins Hotel Dining Room

"I'm sorry, Herr Kipper. We simply cannot provide you with that many three-eighths-inch bolts. The whole next run is already sold, and with the price of iron and steel what they are . . ." Herr Baumgartner said sadly. He was the Grantville representative for several factories in Magdeburg. He, Johan Kipper and Darlene Myers were having dinner in the Higgins Hotel while Johan tried to convince him to up production without upping prices beyond all reason.

"But can't you help us out here, Herr Baumgartner?" Johan asked. "I'm sure that you want to increase production."

"Would that we could, Herr Kipper. We want to help the Prince as much as we can. Look, we are both old Grantville hands. You know how it is. Never enough people, never enough machines, and always more market."

Darlene shook her head in the next best thing to wonder. This wasn't how business worked, she was sure. She had grown up and lived in late-twentieth century America, a world of saturated markets and niche-filling innovation. "Is it really that bad?" she asked.

"I'm not sure 'bad' is the right word." Herr Baumgartner gave her a smile. "It's that way. We are getting rich. Even me, and I am basically a glorified clerk for hire."

Johan laughed a short bark, then turned to Darlene. "Herr Baumgartner is authorized to sign contracts in the name of five corporations in the State of Thuringia-Franconia, and three in the Province of Magdeburg. His 'clerking' involves the transfer of millions of dollars a month."

"But I don't sit on the board of half the companies in Grantville," Herr Baumgartner countered.

"Well, neither do I." Johan grinned at the man. "Herr Baumgartner is a terrible flatterer."

"Why can't you just put on another assembly line if the market is that good?"

"We have. Two, in fact. But it's the cost of steel. USE Steel is producing massive amounts, and now Sweden and Essen have increased their production as well. But the market for it has grown faster. I blame the railroads. I know they say they are necessary, but they gobble up mountains of steel for every mile of track, and there are a lot of miles."

The dinner continued and was a mostly pleasant meal, in spite of the fact that Johan didn't get the nuts and bolts he was after.

Over the next few weeks, Darlene got an education in just how pushed the new industrial complex of the Golden Corridor was. There simply were not enough machines to make the parts to make the machines they needed. So craftsmen were working long hours, putting out cranks and gears and things that could be built at a tenth or a hundredth the cost by a machine—if the machines weren't already putting out all they could. Often enough, they were building parts of machines that would take over their jobs just as soon as they were finished.

But that wasn't the worst of it. It wasn't only steel that was in short supply. The shortages included linen, hemp and cotton, glass and copper and tin, wood and pine rosin and . . . well . . . everything. People were living better in places like Grantville and Magdeburg than they had in living memory, and they were producing more as well. But the economy wasn't able to grow as fast as everyone wanted, no matter how hard it was pushed. Most people, even most people in the State of Thuringia-Franconia and Magdeburg Province, were only a little bit better off than they had been before the war. And there was never enough of the new goods to go around.

Johan was constantly on the move up and down the Saale and Elbe rivers, making deals, begging, borrowing, undercutting the competition to get parts to stock the empty shelves of the store in Zielona Góra and the new ones in Magdeburg, Badenburg, and Saxony. Then he was off again, headed for Saxony.

November, 1635
Dresden

"It's good to see you," David said when the army got to Dresden. Johan, in spite of his running around, had gotten there a day ahead of the army and arranged quarters for himself and Master David. They were in a half-curtained alcove in the main tap room of the inn, having a small beer, cabbage soup, and a rye bread.

"You might not think so when you hear the news," Johan said. "I have been scouring the Golden Corridor for excess production capacity we could pull out here, and there isn't much."

"I didn't expect there would be. That's why we are going to have to build the capacity here. Or rather, wherever we stop. I understand we are heading south tomorrow."

"That's not the only problem. We got a lot of investment, sir, but not enough. Not if we are going to be building whole manufacturing centers."

"How much?" David asked and they talked numbers.

The waiter overheard them talking and went back to ask his papa, who owned the inn, what five point two million dollars amounted to in Saxon thalers. His papa almost fainted. By this time, a Saxon thaler was actually worth less than a USE dollar. John George's paper money had devalued the silver coins as well.

November, 1635

David sank down into the chair in Colonel McAdam's office. "*What?*"

"You think I like it? I just got it over the radio." McAdam complained. "Financial constraints and the needs of the army in Poland mean that Third Division's cash funding is being severely limited. We will be getting just enough USE dollars to pay the troops and no silver at all. We are authorized to issue debit chits."

"Script?" David shook his head. "That's going to turn the whole area against us."

"You think I don't know that? I made the same complaint to the army supply corps commander. You want to know what he said? 'Have that bastard Bartley spin straw into gold.' What did you do to piss him off?"

The new army S4 was a Wettin appointee and a member of the Mecklenburg nobility, the most reactionary nobility in Germany. He had also tried to start a sewing machine business. There were now seventeen sewing machine companies in Germany, but the Higgins still had a fifty-two percent market share because they simply produced more and better sewing machines than anyone else. The army S4 had managed to lose his shirt in trying to start up an eighteenth company using virtual slave labor instead of machines.

"Wasn't me. But he blames Karl for his own stupidity, and Adolph did set the CoC on him."

"Well be that as it may, Captain Bartley, get to spinning or I'm going to have to start issuing divisional IOUs."

"Let me think, sir. I'll get back to you."

David told Johan what was going on, then went for a walk around the camp. By the time he had circled the camp, he had an idea. He was also right next to Jeff Higgins' tent.

November, 1635
Jeff Higgins' Tent, Tetschen

"Run that by me again." Colonel Higgins said as David ran down. Jeff shook his head. "I'm having some trouble with the logic involved."

David managed to hide his irritation at Colonel Higgins' forgetting his new rank yet again. He knew Jeff didn't mean anything by it. More importantly, David felt a bit lost, as he often did when other people couldn't follow his financial reasoning. "Well . . ."

He sat up straighter on the stool in a corner of the Hangman Regiment's HQ tent. "Let's try it this way. The key to the whole thing is the new script. What I'm calling the divisional script."

Higgins shook his head again. "Yeah, I got that. But that's also right where my brain goes blank on account of my jaw hits the floor. If I've got this right, you are seriously proposing to issue currency in the name of the Third Division?"

"Exactly. We'll probably need to come up with some sort of clever name for it, though. 'Script' sounds, well, like script."

"Worthless paper, in other words," provided Thorsten Engler. He, like Bartley and Colonel Higgins, was sitting on a stool in the tent. The flying artillery captain was smiling. Unlike Jeff, he found Bartley's unorthodox notions to be quite entertaining.

"Except it won't be," David said. He wasn't sure how to explain it. The idea was too new. It was based on stuff that he had learned from Sarah and in class, even from Franz Kunze and especially David Heesters, an Amsterdam factor. It had to do with the nature of money and he wasn't sure how to explain it in a way that would both make sense and not give these hardened soldiers nightmares for the rest of their lives. "—which is why we shouldn't call it 'script.' "

"Why won't it be worthless?" asked Major Reinhold Fruehauf, who was slouched against one of the tent poles. Fruehauf commanded the regiment's 20th Battalion.

Bartley felt his face tighten into a squint as he tried to puzzle out how to explain, then gave up. "Why won't it be worthless? Because . . . Well, because it'll officially be worth something." Which wasn't true but was as close as he could come on the spur of the moment.

The regiment's other battalion commander cocked a skeptical eyebrow. "According to who, Captain? You? Or even the regiment itself?" *Major Baldwin Eisenhauer, David thought, has a truly magnificent sneer.* "Ha! Try convincing a farmer of that!"

"He's right, I'm afraid," said Thorsten. His face had a sympathetic expression, though, instead of a sneer. Engler intended to become a psychologist after the war; Major Eisenhauer's ambition was to found a brewery. Their personalities reflected the difference.

"I was once one myself," Engler continued. "There is simply no way that a levelheaded farmer is going to view your script—call it whatever you will—as anything other than the usual 'promissory notes' that foraging troops hand out when they aren't just plundering openly. That is to say, not good for anything except wiping your ass."

They accept American dollars readily enough, from Grantville to Amsterdam. But David was lost for how to explain what he meant. "But—but— of *course* it'll be worth something. We'll get it listed as one of the currencies traded on the Grantville and Magdeburg money exchanges. If Mike—uh, General Stearns—calls in some favors, he'll even avoid having it discounted too much." David squared his shoulders. "I remind all of you that they don't call him the 'Prince of Germany' for no reason. I can pretty much guarantee that even without any special effort, money printed and issued by Mike Stearns will trade at a better value than a lot of European currencies."

Now it was the turn of the other officers in the tent to look befuddled.

"Can he even *do* that?" asked Captain Theobold Auerbach. He was the commander of the artillery battery that had been transferred to Jeff's unit from the Freiheit Regiment.

David scratched his head. "Well . . . it's kind of complicated, Theo. First, there's no law on the books that prevents him from doing it."

Auerbach frowned. "I thought the dollar—"

But David was already shaking his head. "No, that's a common misconception. The dollar is issued by the USE and is recognized as its legal tender, sure enough. But no law has ever been passed that makes it the nation's exclusive currency."

"Ah! I hadn't realized that," said Thorsten. The slight frown on his face vanished. "There's no problem then, from a legal standpoint, unless the prime minister or General Torstensson tells him he can't do it. But I don't see any reason to even mention it to anyone outside the division yet. Right now, we're just dealing with our own logistical needs."

The expressions on the faces of all the down-timers in the tent mirrored Engler's. But Jeff Higgins was still frowning.

"I don't get it. You mean to tell me the USE allows any currency to be used within its borders?" He seemed quite aggrieved.

"You're like most up-timers," David said, "especially ones who don't know much history. The situation we have now is no different from what it was for the first seventy-five years or so of the United States—our old one, back in America. There was an official United States currency—the dollar, of course—but the main currency used by most Americans was the Spanish *real*. The name 'dollar' itself comes from the Spanish dollar, a coin that was worth eight *reales*. It wasn't until the Civil War that the U.S. dollar was made the only legal currency."

"I'll be damned," said Jeff. "I didn't know that."

He wasn't in the least bit discomfited. As was true for most Americans, being charged with historical ignorance was like sprinkling water on a duck.

Jeff rose and stretched a little. "What you're saying, in other words, is that there's technically no reason—legal reason, I mean—that the Third Division couldn't issue its own currency."

"That's right."

A frown was back on Captain Auerbach's face. "I can't think of any army that's ever done so, though."

David shrugged. "So? We're doing lots of new things."

"Let's take it to the general," said Jeff, heading for the tent flap. "We haven't got much time, since he's planning to resume the march tomorrow."

∞ ∞ ∞

General Stearns gave a distracted smile, then a big grin. "Sure, let's do it. D'you need me to leave one of the printing presses behind?"

David considered. They were going to need plates and offset printing, but the general's printing presses were among the best that the combination of up-time and down-time tech could manage. They were quite flexible and had good output. "Probably a good idea, sir. I can afford to buy one easily enough. The problem is that I don't know what's available in the area, and we're familiar with the ones the division brought along."

"Done. Anything else you need?"

David and Jeff looked at each other. Then Jeff said: "Well, we need a name for the currency. We don't want to call it script, of course."

The general scowled. "Company script" was pretty much a profane term among West Virginia coal miners. "No, we sure as hell don't," he said forcefully. He scratched his chin for a few seconds, and then smiled.

"Let's call it a 'becky,' " he said. "Third Division beckies."

David wasn't sure that was a good idea. "Gee, sir, I don't know . . . Meaning no offense, but isn't that pushing nepotism a bit far?"

Jeff laughed. "In the year sixteen thirty-five? For Christ's sake, David, nepotism is the most favored middle name around. Most rulers in the here and now get their position by inheritance, remember?"

"Well, yeah, but . . ."

The general's grin faded a little. "Relax, Captain. The problem with nepotism is that it can lead to incompetence and it's often tied to corruption. But neither of those issues are involved here. It's just a name, that's all."

David thought about it for a moment. "Okay, I can see that." After another moment of thought, he added, "And now that I think about it, naming the division's unit of currency after your own wife is likely to boost confidence in it. The here and now being the way it is."

∞ ∞ ∞

The army stopped at the border between Saxony and Bohemia for a couple of days to get organized. Jeff Higgins was left in charge of the border post while General Stearns and the rest of the army proceeded south to Prague.

Johan didn't know until the general had left that David and General Stearns had decided to introduce their own money. Third Division beckies, of all things. He wasn't at all comfortable with the idea of the Prince of Germany issuing money, but he did concede that if they were going to do it, putting the face of a Jewess on it was going to reassure people.

"Where are we going to get the goods to sell and trade for supplies?" Johan asked. "I know you've been on the radio and I have been working my sources as well, but still . . ."

"I know," David told Johan. "But I think we may have a way around that problem, at least part of it . . . if we can get some production machines, even a few. Look, I have the clothing company back in Grantville and I can divert most of its output to us. And we can get some of the lathes and we are close to the river, so until it freezes up . . ."

Johan shook his head. "There was ice on the water before I got to Dresden. Delivery is going to be overland and sleighs, probably. And remember, Saxony has just been through a change of government. It's not the most settled place in the USE."

"What I was thinking is we can set up some businesses here, using the local resources and some of the men as a work force. We can start producing stuff. Parts . . . I don't know what all yet. But we know how to start companies to make stuff. And, Johan, they need stuff here. All sorts of stuff. It's almost as though the Ring of Fire never happened, and we're what? A hundred miles from Grantville?"

"More like a hundred and fifty as the crow flies, I think. And perhaps twice that, as the caravan moves."

"Well, the roads are improved?" David's voice sounded hopeful.

"Not around here, they aren't. There are maybe forty miles of consistent good road in this direction from Grantville and I wouldn't trust even that if we get any sort of heavy snows. The rest of it . . . well, some of the villages have bought or built scrapers and improved the little stretch of road next to them, but a lot haven't. And you know your transport is determined by what can get over the worst bit of road, not what can travel on the best."

David used a bit of coarse language at that point, though nothing that Johan hadn't already heard. Most of it learned from Johan, probably.

But that didn't change the facts. "That's going to make the whole money thing harder and, at the same time, more important."

"How do you mean?"

"The less we can bring in over bad roads, the more we will have to buy locally and we aren't going to have much to buy it with besides the beckies."

"What about American dollars, or silver, for that matter?"

"Silver, maybe. But the truth is, I don't think the American dollar . . ." David paused and tried to put his gut feeling into words. From the attitudes of the people hereabout, the problem wasn't that they didn't trust the American dollar. It was more like they didn't see a lot of difference between a USE dollar and a Prince of Germany dollar. A USE dollar wasn't a John George thaler that was worthless, but it wasn't silver, either. Whose money they could trust was a matter of concern to them, but the up-timers seemed to be the good money people, more even than the USE was. "I don't think there's much difference—in the minds of these people—between American dollars and beckies. In fact, beckies might seem more American than bucks."

"So it's all going to come down to what we have to sell?"

"At first, yes."

∞ ∞ ∞

While the artist was working on the design of the becky, Johan and David worked on making sure they had something to sell. There were problems with that, though. Not the least of which was transportation.

November, 1635
Unnamed Village, East of Wilkau

"You want what?" the village head man asked.

"We want you to improve the road between here and Wolkenstein." Lieutenant Lucco Ponte was just starting out on this project, based on a radio message from Johan Kipper. The roads, once you got into Saxony, sucked. Still. After almost four years. And Lucco, at the ripe old age of nineteen, thought it was disgusting. He had, with great rapidity, become an adherent of all things up-time: hot showers every day, cologne, safety razors, and—especially—good clothing a man could afford. But now he was back in the seventeenth century and he didn't like it one little bit. He didn't understand why these people hadn't put together a fresno scraper and improved the local roads on their own.

"Why should we?" the village head man asked. The man was dressed in third-hand homespun, hadn't had a shower in some time and had clearly never even heard of cologne or deodorant in general. He had also eaten something with very strong onions for dinner a day or so ago. As far as Lucco was concerned, the man reeked.

Lucco held his breath for a moment, then explained. "So that wagons can come through and you will have access to goods from the factories."

"Don't have the money," the head man said, and Lucco wasn't sure whether he was referring to the money to improve the road or the money to buy the goods. Perhaps both.

"You'll also be able to get more money for your crops."

"Don't trust your up-timer paper."

Lucco looked at the man in shock. They were . . . he really wasn't all that sure exactly how far from Grantville. He had taken a morning to get to Jena on the train, then the evening riding a good horse over good roads to get to Zwickau. Then, the next morning he had followed still pretty good roads to Wilkau and a bit beyond, where the road turned into a trail to this place—which was apparently bound and determined to stay mired in the seventeenth, or perhaps sixteenth, century.

"Why under heaven not?"

"It's paper," the man told him, as though that explained everything.

"So what? You're not going to eat it. You're going to spend it."

"You like it so much, you take it."

Tobias Hagemann looked at the young dandy in the fancy clothing and felt something between fear and contempt. The . . . boy . . . was well-dressed, even considerably over-dressed, and he was armed. That's where the fear came from. But he was a boy and enamored of the up-timers. Tobias had never met an up-timer and wasn't in any hurry to. There was no radio in the village. Someone tried to sell them one a couple of years back, but they had run the witch out of town. Tobias still wasn't sure they had done enough just running him out of town. The book said you shouldn't suffer a witch to live, and voices through the ether, that was witchcraft, sure enough.

Still, the effects of the up-timers were felt here, even if indirectly. There were goods available in Zwickau for ridiculously low prices and some of the villagers had taken to going there to buy things. But that was no reason to improve the road. If anything, to Tobias' mind, it was reason not to. "Look, mister, I don't want your road. I don't need your road, and the Elector is going to deal with you."

"John George is dead. Has been for months. Don't you people have radios?"

"No, we don't. We don't hold with witchcraft here. And we know how to deal with witches."

Tobias froze then, because at his last statement the young dandy's hand had dropped to the butt of what was clearly a gun. But not like any gun Tobias had ever seen.

"Radios are not witchcraft," the young dandy said, and suddenly he seemed a lot less contemptible.

"They are technology. Knowledge put to use. Anyone can make them and they require no spells or incantations, nor any deal with any demonic power to work. Like guns." The dandy patted the butt of his firearm. "Or water wheels. Just devices made by men using the knowledge and ability God gave us all."

∞ ∞ ∞

Lucco was frightened when the old man started talking about witchcraft. Partly because he had felt the same way only a few years before and he realized just how easily such an attitude could get out of hand. His hand slipped, without thought, to the forty-five caliber revolver that he carried on his hip, and that reassuring presence let him explain to the old fart that radios weren't witchcraft.

"Look, sir," Lucco continued after he had told the old man about radios, "I am not trying to tell you how to live your life, but there's a big world out there and it's not going to ignore you forever, no matter what you or I want. We need a way to get goods to Tetschen, on the border between Saxony and Bohemia."

Then he saw the gleam in the old fart's eyes. He knew that the old man was thinking of tolls. He carefully forbore to mention that military supplies didn't pay taxes or tolls by USE law.

Since the likelihood of any attack on the State of Thuringia-Franconia was close to nil now that Saxony was out of the picture, Ponte Company would probably get the job of transporting supplies. He had heard rumors of a possible attack from Bavaria but that was patently ridiculous.

November, 1635
Chabařovice, Bohemia

Most of the way to Tetschen, Johan Kipper and Sergeant Beckmann were in a village with a similar attitude. Chabařovice, it seemed, didn't care for the village of Jílové some eleven miles and two villages away. "They are all cheats, every last one of them, and pig thieves. Forty years ago Paulus Hebeber stole the widow Trunck's pig and they have yet to make restitution. We won't improve the road to those people and we are in Bohemia, so you can't make us."

The shortest route to Teplitz from Tetschen would be through a valley that went west from Tetschen. However, the feuding towns were in the way and neither one of them wanted a road to the other. Johan shook his head. "Just as you say then. We will take a different route."

November, 1635
Ústí nad Labem, Bohemia

The different route they ended up taking led them to the Elbe at a place called Ústí nad Labem, about fourteen and a half miles southwest of Tetschen. The distance from Teplitz to Tetschen by that route was about twenty-five miles rather than the twenty-two that it would have been if they had been able to go through Chabařovice and Jilove. In latter years, the feud between the two towns would expand to include the lack of the road, each town blaming the other for blocking the road.

From Teplitz to Litvinov, the roads were already quite good, passing through two villages with a side road to a third. All of them ten feet or better wide, with gravel capable of supporting wagon traffic. From Litvinov to Seiffen proved more difficult, not because of obstreperous villagers, but because of the terrain. The border between Saxony and Bohemia was where it was for a reason. A ridge line stretches between

199

Saxony and Bohemia and the road had to make its way over the ridge. There were two decent routes, through Kliny and through Deutschneudorf. Deutschneudorf was the larger town and was in Saxony, but it was also very insistent on using its drovers for any transport on its roads. Kliny, on the other hand, was a small town with a much more accommodating attitude. Probably because they were part of King Albrecht Wallenstein's personal fief and he had told them to be. But accommodating attitude or not, the hills were still hills and it was still freezing out. The fresnos were scraping a lot more snow than earth. Snow roads are workable . . . until you get a warm day and they melt. And even in winter in the Little Ice Age, there was the occasional warm day.

November, 1635
Kliny, Bohemia

"Why are we doing all this again?" Sergeant Beckmann asked as they sat in a house in Kliny, the king of Bohemia not being in residence just at the moment. Actually, the king, to the best of Johan's knowledge, had never been in Kliny. There was, however, some sort of family connection.

"We are setting up a transport route to get goods from the golden corridor to Tetschen," Johan said.

"Sure. But why? We could sell the stuff we are going to be selling in Tetschen a lot closer, at a good profit. Why go to all the trouble to take them all the way to Tetschen?"

"Because we aren't just making a profit on the goods. We are making a profit on the money too." This one had confused Johan at first, but it was true. As long as beckies circulated, they were, in effect, a free loan to the Third Division. And even if it was a fairly short-term loan that was constantly getting repaid, there were going to be enough beckies to produce a considerable profit. "But we only make that extra money if the beckies are accepted as good money. And, in the long run, that only works if they *are* good money. So, to make them good money, we have to make sure that they will buy stuff. And to do that, we have to have stuff to sell where the division is."

Beckmann dropped his head to the table. "This makes no sense."

Johan grinned a very insincere grin. "Trust me."

Chapter 15—Rate of Exchange

December, 1635
Gorndorf

"Where the hell have you been, Lucco?" Captain Ponte was apparently not thrilled.

"I've been arranging to improve the roads between here and Tetschen. Just like you told me to."

"You were supposed to be back two weeks ago."

"I would have been, but every half-mile I had to stop and negotiate with another village council. Every damned farmer between Zwickau and Tetschen had to have his say before the roads could be turned from a goat path to something a wagon could travel on."

"Well, that idiot in Bavaria has attacked Ingolstadt and we are moving south."

"What? That's crazy!"

"And Maximillian is known for his sanity?"

Lucco didn't have any answer for that. "What about finishing and transporting the big order for winter gear?"

"The ladies are hiring extra help." Captain Ponte grimaced at his little brother. "We are going to have to leave the women here alone."

"Is that safe?"

"Safer than taking them with us. And besides, we have to get the winter gear that the boss diverted to Tetschen and the Third Division."

"We could claim that the roads prevented our transporting it and sell it to the State of Thuringia-Franconia Guard, the way we planned."

"Not a good idea to piss off Captain Bartley."

Lucco snorted. "I'd a lot rather piss off Bartley than Kipper."

"Nope. Piss off Kipper and you just have to deal with Kipper. He's not likely to take it to Bartley. But piss off Bartley and you have them both to deal with."

"Well, I don't see how we are going to get them through. Not without us along to guard the caravans. Every village on the route is going to charge them duty on everything they carry, and they will run out of money and goods before they ever reach Tetschen."

"I don't know, either," Captain Ponte said.

December, 1635
Rudolstadt

Gerlach Transport was the very old pickup truck that Peter Gerlach bought at a hugely inflated price in 1632. He then spent even more money having the old junker fixed and converted to use natural gas. In fact, he had bought as many tanks for natural gas as he could find, so the bed of the pickup was full of tanks, giving the sucker considerable range. That truck, along with a train of two trailers it pulled, could carry over ten tons of cargo at an average speed of fifteen miles an hour over dirt roads. His tires had snow chains on them and were filled with tar, not air, so they wouldn't go flat. Peter and his wife did the driving and slept in a space he had built over the gas tanks. It was a small company, but it made a good living shipping loads of cargo over the good roads around the Ring of Fire, and increasingly, through northern Thuringia-Franconia. He looked up at the two men who had just come into his office at his home base, just on the far side of Rudolstadt from the Ring of Fire. "Can I help you?"

"Are you available for a larger transport job?"

"Yes, as it happens. Winter is a slow time."

"We need you to take goods from the railhead at Jena to Tetschen in Bohemia."

Peter shook his head. "The roads won't take the truck."

"They will now, or at least they will soon."

"What are you talking about?"

"We are from the Ponte Clothing Company and we have been arranging with the villages along the route to improve the roads."

Peter had heard that sort of claim before and learned to take it with considerably more than a grain of salt. "I would have to examine the road before I could make any promises. Besides, there is the question of what will I be bringing back. What do they have in this Tetschen place that is worth shipping to the rail head at Jena?"

∞ ∞ ∞

It took a few days before Peter Gerlach had time to go up and see the road. And when he did he wasn't impressed. Sure it was wide enough to run his rig, but not if there was traffic going the other way. Someone would have to get off the road and there was no place on most of the road to pull over to the side and let someone pass. Not that that was an unusual circumstance. His truck and trailer rig was wider than most down-time wagons by a good two feet, and it was less forgiving of bumpy sidings than the high wheels and especially high axles of a wagon.

∞ ∞ ∞

While all that was going on, David Bartley was burning up the airways with messages to his factor in Magdeburg and his friends in Magdeburg and Grantville. It was late December when the beckies were listed on the Grantville Exchange. They were offered at par with the New USE dollar and several people were in attendance.

December, 1635
Grantville Stock Exchange

Gertrude Schmidt talked with her sister Hilda and watched the board. When the beckies came up, offered at a price of one becky to one USE dollar, she called over one of the clerks and put in an order for five thousand of them.

The clerk nodded and smiled. He had been expecting her order. Everyone in the room knew that the beckies were Third Division scrip and that Mike Stearns and David Bartley were both putting their reputations on the line for them. It was only to be expected that their friends would buy a few in solidarity.

In the case of the Schmidt family, it was even arranged. Gertrude's buy of five thousand was joined by others. Dave Marcantonio and Ollie Rearden bought some, apparently out of personal friendship for Mike Stearns. The financial agent for the Grantville High School bought some, more for political than financial reasons. In just a few minutes the twenty thousand beckies that had been offered had all been bought.

"That went better than I expected," Gertrude told her next younger sister, Hilda.

"You were being silly. Who wants to be known as the one who didn't buy a becky?"

"Sure, but not everyone has to buy one, and you don't really expect them to maintain par with the American dollar."

"The beckies are as much American dollars as the USE dollars are," Hilda said. "They are backed by Mike Stearns, not Wettin and Oxenstierna."

"Axel Oxenstierna has nothing to do with the USE dollar and Prime Minister Wettin doesn't have much."

"Right. Pull the other one," Hilda said. "Wettin does whatever Oxenstierna says, or what is he doing in Berlin? Answer me that. And Wettin appoints the Secretary of the Treasury. And the head of the Federal Reserve Bank of the USE. You watch. One of Oxenstierna's cronies will end up in charge of the Fed and another will be head of Treasury."

"Treasury, maybe. But the Fed Chair is appointed for a four-year term. And Walker was only appointed last year," Gertrude insisted. "Even if he wanted to, Wettin couldn't replace him for three years. Thank goodness."

"Maybe, but a Fed Chair can be removed for malfeasance and I wouldn't put it past Wettin to have him impeached."

"On what grounds?"

"Failure to trim his toenails properly. It's votes, not guilt or innocence that would decide."

Hilde had a rare talent, Gertrude thought, of taking a really pleasant day and turning it into crap.

December, 1635
Between Tetschen and Zwickau

"It's the prices," Johan told Beckmann for the third time.

"So you've said, but Mast . . . ah, Captain Bartley has friends and he is buying in the golden corridor, or at least his agents are."

"That's right, but . . ." Johan paused. "It's supply and demand. The demand has been growing faster than supply since the day of the Ring of Fire. And every foot of improved road or railroad, every balloon, every airplane, every barge and boat, increases the demand even more. That's pushing prices up, or would be if there was enough money."

"It *is* pushing prices up. A pair of vice grips is going for a *reichsthaler* and that's in Magdeburg."

"Or sixty dollars each, bought by the gross, but even so, the only reason that it's not a case of too few goods is because there aren't enough dollars. There just aren't enough businesses making things."

Sergeant Beckmann looked at Johan like he was crazy. "I've been to Magdeburg. They are making more stuff in that damn town than in Paris, Amsterdam, London and Rome all put together."

"Yep, and it's not enough." They were in another village on the road—such as it was—between Tetschen and Zwickau. And the village leaders were sitting around the same table, listening to them.

"Do they really make so much?" asked one. "We hear on the radio, but it seems so far and not quite real."

"Yes, they really make that much. And it's really that little. Not nearly enough for all the people who could put it to good use," Johan said, then turned back to Beckmann. "That's why the beckies. Because we need more factories and it takes money to build the machines for the new factories. Any village could make itself a good living if it could scrape together the money to buy a stamp forge and maybe a steam lathe."

Suddenly they were even more the center of attention in the village. "What do you mean?" Georg Michael, the village leader asked. He was a man of late middle-age with some trouble breathing, but he didn't let that stop him from working.

"Well, once the road comes through here, it will be relatively cheap to ship goods to the Elbe at Tetschen and then to the rail head at Jena. So you could manufacture tools and ship them out for sale. Like the vice grips that Sergeant Beckmann here was complaining about. With a drop forge for basic shaping and a lathe and borer for finishing, you could make vice grips. And like he said, they are going for a *reichsthaler* apiece in Magdeburg. More, around here. Not that you would get that. You would use up the local sales pretty quickly, but shipping to the store we are setting up in Tetschen or the store back in Zielona Góra gives you an outlet for them.

And it's not just the vice grips. Almost any tool has a market. Almost anything of any sort has a market. Plowshares, for instance. Knives. For that matter, forks and spoons and nails and screws and bolts and nuts. There's never enough of anything."

"But who can buy it?" Georg Michael asked. "We have barely enough to make ends meet now and, well, no offense, but I don't trust paper money."

"You would if you had been to Grantville," Beckmann said, smiling.

It doesn't matter," Johanna, Georg Michael's wife said. "We don't have the money to buy a drop forge or those other things you talked about."

"A loan might be arranged," Sergeant Beckmann said.

"Don't like debt!" Georg said firmly.

Johan and Beckmann let it drop and turned the conversation to other things. You couldn't make people move into the new world if they weren't ready to come, and a lot of them weren't.

December, 1635
Tetschen

"What's the status of the roads?" David asked when Johan and Beckmann got back.

"Improving. I suspect we will be able to bring the goods through without more than standard delays. By the time we have some goods to move, that is. How have you been doing raising funds?"

"Pretty well. The new beckies are being printed and they are official. Trading on the money markets in Magdeburg and Grantville. Amsterdam and Venice haven't picked them up yet, but that's probably for the best. Amsterdam isn't all that thrilled with the dollar and are seriously discounting the USE dollar. I figure they would do the same to the becky, only worse."

"And Venice is still uncomfortable with paper money," Johan agreed. "What's the situation in Dresden?"

"Banér has invested the city, or he's doing so. We haven't heard as much as I would like but I think it's going to prove a really good thing that we have another supply route."

"Is he crazy?" Beckmann asked.

"I think he must have at least tacit permission from someone," David said.

Technically, what Banér was doing could be called putting down an uprising. Except for the fact that there was no uprising to put down. But that probably wasn't how Banér saw it. To him, the CoC acting to insure order was an uprising.

"So what are we going to do?" Beckmann asked.

"General Stearns is still in Bohemia talking to Wallenstein. I have no idea what he has in mind. What I think he should do is bring Third Division back here and kick Banér's ass."

"That might not be the most politically astute move," Johan said with great and obvious diplomacy.

David snorted. "Was I being just a bit too bloody-minded there, Johan?"

"A condition of youth, Master David," Johan said with a grin.

David grimaced a bit but got back to business. "What about the winter uniforms? We got some before Banér cut the road, but what about the rest?"

Johan could only shrug.

December, 1635
On the road to Zwickau

Peter Gerlach sat hunched over the steering wheel with the heater turned all the way up and the wipers pushing snow and sleet off the windshield. He was making perhaps five miles per hour and had been for the last two hours. That was because of a sudden snowstorm that caught them about halfway between Jena and Zwickau. So far the roads had been fine; it was the weather that had been a killer. This was a big load. Both trailers were filled to capacity with uniforms, as were the sleeping quarters above the tanks. He and Maria, his wife, were even wearing a set each, thanks to Ponte Clothing. They were warm enough that they both had unbuttoned the jackets.

The drifting snow obscured his vision for a moment and he was almost caught by the turn. He braked a little hard and the truck slid a foot or so, in spite of the chains. But they were creeping along in their lowest gear, and the transmission had been reworked to give them really low gears, so they didn't slide far.

Peter cursed and Maria whacked him on the shoulder. "What are you complaining about? I am the one who's going to have to go out in that to guide you around the corner."

Over the last year Peter and Maria had worked out a detailed set of signals that let them instruct each other on how they needed to turn the truck to make sure that both trailers stayed on the road. It wasn't an easy thing to do, but they had driven a lot of hours in all sorts of conditions. They were good at their job.

Maria buttoned up and opened the passenger door, then slipped and slid around the truck to the front, where she looked over the situation. Then she had him back up about a foot and a half, then shift to the right a little to adjust the turning arc of the first trailer. For the next fifteen minutes, they backed and shifted till the road train could get around the too-sharp corner. And the next one, which was only about fifty feet further.

Marie had icicles on her coat when she climbed back aboard the truck. "I think my eyeballs are frozen."

Three more hours and they finally made Zwickau. What should have taken three hours had taken ten, and they needed a place to stay. Their little cubbyhole over the truck bed was filled with uniforms and way too cold in this weather anyway.

Climbing out of the truck, they headed for the largest building in the town, which was an inn. Zwickau was on the border between the State of Thuringia-Franconia and Saxony, so there had been considerable trade through there since before Saxony had seceded from the newly formed USE. That trade had continued with no noticeable interruption all during the aborted secession and only increased after John George was removed, so there was a regular market and an inn to facilitate travel and trade.

The next morning, the world was white and shiny, covered with a blanket of snow with a thin crust of ice on top of it. The snow crackled as Peter made his way out to the truck and he had to bang on the truck to loosen the sleet coating enough to open the door. Once he got into the cab, he started up the truck and checked his fuel level. The converted 1987 Ford F-series started in spite of the cold but Peter took good care of it. He went back into the inn while the engine warmed up.

Fifteen minutes and a bucket of water later, the windshield was clear of sleet and Peter and Maria were on their way, crunching through the snow. They made moderate time that day, covering about forty miles in seven hours and stopped in the town of Seiffen. Seiffen was a mining town, but the mines had mostly played out by this time, though they were hoping that up-time mining techniques would let them find new veins of ore.

Which was what Peter and Maria heard about that evening, though Maria did notice some of the really nice carvings that were made locally.

On the third day in the afternoon, they reached the Army base in Tetschen and unloaded the uniforms at the castle on the hill.

"We were starting to get a little worried," Captain David Bartley said, while Peter was still getting out of the cab. "What was the delay?"

"A snow storm our first day out. We had to go slowly and carefully. We still had to go slowly and carefully after it had passed, because snow drifts were covering the road in a lot of places.

"We were told there would be a cargo back?"

"Yes. It's a mixed bag. Tetschen is a trade center, or it was before it got burned down. And there is a bit of everything down-time made in its warehouses. Here is a manifest. Most of it should sell in Grantville, though it's not as high a value as what you will be bringing this way."

That set the tone. Peter and Maria spent a day in Tetschen unloading uniforms and loading cargo for Grantville and then headed out the next morning. Two or three days each way, carrying several tons, and it was looking to be a busy winter. Especially since winter is hard on mules. Two more trips of uniforms and then they started carrying lathes and other up-time manufacturing equipment to turn Tetschen into a minor manufacturing center.

January, 1636
Tetschen

"How are the beckies doing?" Johan asked a few days after the last of the uniforms arrived.

"So so. We will do better as we get in more goods from Grantville and the corridor to sell."

∞ ∞ ∞

They got the order to move not long after that. Except for David and a couple of hundred supply personnel, who were ordered to stay in Tetschen and maintain the supplies while the Hangman Regiment moved out. Then Mike Stearns showed up and repeated the order. David and the supply units would stay in Tetschen and hand out uniforms while the rest of the army passed through on its way to Dresden to deal with Banér.

"I literally get to stay here and hold the army's coats while they come through to go to the fight," David said, trying to make it sound like a joke, but not doing a great job.

"You aren't missing anything worth seeing," Johan told him seriously.

January, 1636
Higgins Hotel, Grantville

"Reports are that Third Division is moving north to relieve Dresden from Banér's siege," the radio blared.

Darlene started panicking the moment she heard the radio report. Johan was with Third Division. And what would she do without him now that she'd found him? She had already lost one husband and son, taken away by the Ring of Fire.

That thought stopped her.

In a perfectly safe world with damn few ways of losing your loved ones, the Ring of Fire had come along and taken her family. And she was worried about a war in the seventeenth century?

It wasn't that she stopped worrying about the war. It was more that the very existence of the Ring of Fire proved that all safety was illusion. Still, there were levels of risk, and being scooped up by the Ring of Fire had to rank in probability somewhere below being hit by a meteorite. Whereas getting your fool head shot off because you left your wife and baby to run off to war when you damned well ought to be old enough to know better was a much more likely outcome. Having determined that Johan was an unfeeling idiot, she managed to regain her equilibrium somewhat. She was still worried, but there wasn't anything she could do about it.

She picked up her son and hugged him. "Your daddy is a jerk, Hans, and you're going to grow up to be one too. You can't help it. It's that Y chromosome. It does it to all of you. I can't even point it out to him by asking about a will, because he already had one made up as soon as we got married and then he updated it as soon as we knew you were coming. The jerk. You're set for life, even if he does get himself killed chasing after the Bartley boy. And so am I. Darn it."

The baby gurgled happily at her, already taking the male side.

"And I'm outnumbered. I need to have a little girl to balance things out. But I'd have to get your daddy back here to do his part. But knowing Johan, it would probably be another boy. It's always the man's fault if it's a boy. It's a scientific fact."

There was laughter from the door, and Maria came in. "It's their fault if it's a girl too, as I pointed out to my husband before he went off to war."

"I don't know why we put up with them," Darlene complained, only partly in jest.

"I do," Maria said with a salacious grin.

Darlene snorted. "What is on the agenda for today?"

"You are going to work and I am taking these two to the Play Room." The Higgins Hotel had several children in residence, so it possessed a daycare center of its own, called the Play Room. The Play Room had a variety of educational toys suitable for children from infants to school age. It was generally well populated.

"We could take them to Twinlo Park."

"It's cold out there." Maria shook her head. "Really cold."

Which was true enough. Twinlo Park had a daycare center but taking the babies out into the cold to go from one daycare center to another daycare center seemed a pretty silly thing to do. So, with regret, Darlene turned Hans David over to the nanny and headed off to work.

January, 1636
Village on the road to Eisenach

"I assure you, Frau, this is the best deal we can possibly offer," said Herr Junker, with a smile that made Darlene want to hide her jewelry.

But they had been going over this for the last half hour, and she was afraid that she had actually been losing ground in the bargaining. "Very well, Herr Junker, I will have my lawyers go over the agreement and get back to you."

"As you wish," Herr Junker said. "But I assure you, the contract is perfectly valid."

The issue was a small farming village about ten miles the other side of Badenburg, on the road to Eisenach. Darlene had talked with Johan about buying the rents on a village as sort of a country estate, close enough to Grantville to make it an easy day trip but far enough to be quiet and peaceful. They figured on building a house out there as a place for the crumbsnatcher, and any little brother or sister that happened along, to play and grow up. Landed gentry with a country estate, that was what they were going to be whenever Johan got through following David Bartley into battles.

"I'm sure it is." Darlene gave him her best dumb blonde look. "But Johan would be so upset if I didn't have his lawyer look at it." There was no way Darlene was going to sign a contract written in German without having a down-time lawyer look it over, but there was no reason to take the heat if she could put it on Johan—who wasn't even here to complain.

"Of course, Frau Myers." Herr Junker, who was a cousin of the Badenburg Junkers but lived in Eisenach, almost managed to not look disappointed . . . but only almost.

Darlene looked around the village again. It was a fair-sized village. Almost fifty families had lived here before the war and quite a few moved back after the area stabilized. Probably, with up-time tech, they only needed about five families to run the place, but Darlene had been talking with them and figured she and Johan could help the tenants shift to manufacturing. It was a nice place, and she was getting it for a great price.

Chapter 16—Taking Care of the Up-timers

January, 1636
Tetschen

For the next weeks, David divided his time between dodging the daughters of the local gentry and reassuring their fathers that in spite of the fact that most of Third Division had gone, they weren't facing imminent ruin.

"You're not thinking it through, sir," David told one of the fathers. "Yes, the Third is gone, but you are well located. Spring will be here soon, the river route will open up, and goods will flow again. Meanwhile, with the road improvements, there are goods coming in. And you are right on the border between Bohemia and the USE. Goods from both countries will come through here. You're in an excellent position to make considerable profits, not just on the finished goods but on goods manufactured right here from materials brought in."

David looked at his records for a minute. "Look, you have access to manufactured goods from the whole corridor, and you have the Jena road, which goes through a lot of farming villages which are producing wool and rye and beans. Set up some canneries, a few freeze-drying plants. Sell preserved foods. I know cans are still expensive, but you can get some good freeze dryers from Magdeburg. I know the man that makes the best of them. Wallenstein will want freeze-dried food for his armies and so will

General Stearns. Talk to your neighbors, get the local roads improved so that people can ship goods here cheaply and you can process them."

The eyes of the father of a particularly vapid example of Bohemian gentry were glazing with visions of great wealth, and those visions weren't entirely fairy dust. Production was still very concentrated in the golden corridor, but this was arguably the north edge of that corridor. At least till Morris Roth got things in Bohemia a little more under control, and even when he did, that would only mean that there would be more goods going both ways—right through here. The same terrain that made this place the place you wanted to win if you were going to invade Bohemia or Saxony also made it the natural place to get rich off the trade between the two nations.

"Yes, yes," said the man. "That could work."

"Maybe if we had the money," said his partner, whose daughter was quite bright and not the least interested—*thank God*—in David and who had helped fend off some of the more insistent parents. Julia, the girl in question, was as it happened, quite interested in one Major David Barclay and David wished her good luck in her pursuit. Which would have to be done by mail for the next little while because Major Barclay was with most of the Third Division in Dresden. Well, camped outside it. All of which proved that she had come by her smarts legitimately.

"But when you leave, Major Bartley, you will be taking your bank?" His hopeful tone made it a question.

"And the beckies?" David smiled. "No. We will be leaving the Third Division Exchange store and bank right here. It will be operated by veterans of the Third Division, but there were some lost in the battle for Dresden. Quite a few wounded soldiers in need of work. Some of them will be coming back here just as soon as they can be moved. The bank and the beckies will be here, just as they are even now being made available in Poland."

"So we can get loans to keep the businesses busy until we can start selling our goods upriver?"

"Yes, I think some loans can be arranged."

But finally, a few days after his talk with the fathers of Tetschen's eligible daughters, David managed to escape. The Third Division was going to kick Maximilian out of Ingolstadt and keep right on kicking 'till he was removed from Munich as well. And, wonder of wonders, they were going to need supplies.

March, 1636
Grantville

David Bartley, in winter uniform, came off the train first. Much of the army was marching south, but David and Johan had business to take care of here in Grantville. Most of the workers in his clothing factory—or sweatshop, as he thought of it—had been activated and headed south while the Third Division was still in Tetschen. They hired replacements, but hiring people near Grantville was expensive. So he and Johan were looking at ways to either get more people to come from outside the area or to move the factory up to the Elbe, where transport was cheaper. There were also about a hundred other matters of business to manage, some personal, some for the division.

"I am still amazed how well the beckies are doing. Sure, out in the boonies where they are the only decent currency available, but in Grantville and Magdeburg?" David Barclay was telling David Bartley as they detrained. Barclay had taken a few days off to handle the investments of his regiment.

"Honestly, so am I," David Bartley admitted. "But as long as they are, we need to get industrial capacity up in the places where we have the Exchange stores, so there will be products to trade for them. I don't like having to get everything from the golden corridor."

Their conversation was interrupted by a plump female missile. David and David looked back to see short, stocky Johan Kipper almost bowled over by a short, stocky Darlene Myers. "Don't break him, Darlene," David said. "He's really quite useful."

Darlene paid David no attention. Which was only fair. He shook his head as Darlene hauled Johan off on some errand. Clearly, David wasn't the only one who had business that needed handling in Grantville. David just wished his business was a little more like Johan's.

March, 1636
Kipper Suite, Higgins Hotel

"I had a talk with Dieter Junker. The contract will be rewritten, and we will pay a fairer rate for the rents and get more of the rights as well," Johan said in a condescending tone.

That was what really pissed Darlene off. She hadn't thought of Johan as a male chauvinist pig till this. But he sounded just like a guy back up-time, telling her he had gotten a better deal at the car dealership. No, come to think of it, it wasn't just the tone of voice. It was the fact that he had gotten the village and better fishing and hunting rights, all for less. A lot less. "Yes, dear," she gritted out.

Johan patted her shoulder and went past her to play with little Hans. It was a challenge for Darlene not to brain him with a cast iron skillet. She had to get out of there. "I'm going to go up and say hi to Delia."

That's fine, dear." He didn't even look up.

March, 1636
Penthouse, Higgins Hotel

"He follows your grandkid around like a puppy and treats me like I'm an idiot. I thought we were in the seventeenth century, not Victorian England."

Delia laughed.

David grinned and shook his head. "No, Darlene, you don't understand. Johan is indeed very loyal to me and our family. He considers us very good and noble people, in the up-time sense of the word. But he hadn't been in Grantville a week before he decided that none of us were actually competent to look after ourselves in the real world. So he has a tendency to manage us all, as servants have been doing all through history all over the world."

"What does that have to . . . "

"The reason he sometimes treats you like you're not quite capable of wiping your backside isn't because you're a woman. It's because you're an up-timer."

The End

Made in the USA
Middletown, DE
04 November 2019